Mystery of the
Missing Stallions

ALSO BY RUTH NULTON MOORE

For Junior High Readers
Danger in the Pines
The Ghost Bird Mystery
In Search of Liberty
Mystery at Indian Rocks
Mystery of the Lost Treasure
Peace Treaty
The Sorrel Horse
Wilderness Journey

For Younger Readers
Tomás and the Talking Birds
Tomás y los Pajaros Párlantes (Spanish)

Mystery of the Missing Stallions

Ruth Nulton Moore

Illustrated by James Converse

Sara and Sam Series, Book 1

HERALD PRESS
Scottdale, Pennsylvania
Kitchener, Ontario
1984

Library of Congress Cataloging in Publication Data

Moore, Ruth Nulton.
  Mystery of the missing stallions.

  (Sara and Sam series ; bk. 1)
  Summary: Teenage twins Sara and Sam investigate a
young Vietnamese refugee hiding in an abandoned cabin
and the mysterious disappearance of thoroughbred stallions
from a neighbor's horse farm.
  [1. Twins—Fiction.   2. Vietnamese Americans—
Fiction.   3. Mystery and detective stories]
I. Converse, James, ill.   II. Title.   III. Series:
Moore, Ruth Nulton. Sara and Sam series ; bk. 1.
PZ7.M7878Mz   1984   [Fic]   84-19764
ISBN 0-8361-3376-5 (pbk.)

MYSTERY OF THE MISSING STALLIONS
Copyright © 1984 by Herald Press, Scottdale, Pa. 15683
  Published simultaneously in Canada by Herald Press,
  Kitchener, Ont. N2G 4M5
Library of Congress Catalog Card Number: 84-19764
International Standard Book Number: 0-8361-3376-5
Printed in the United States of America
Design by Alice B. Shetler

90 89 88 87 86 85 84 10 9 8 7 6 5 4 3 2 1

To my Granddaughter
Lindsay Ruth Moore
with love

Contents

1
A New Home

HOW long before we reach Maplewood?" Sam Harmon asked, straightening up from his slouch and resting his elbows on the back of the front seat of the station wagon. He twisted his wrist to consult his new digital watch. "We should be getting there soon, shouldn't we?"

His sister Sara, who was sitting in the front seat next to their mother, glanced over at the odometer and made a mental calculation. "Ten more miles, Sam."

"I know we'll all like living in Maplewood," Mrs. Harmon told them as she slowed down for a truck. "It's a quaint college town, and your father and I fell in love with it the first time we saw it."

"But we won't be living right in Maplewood," Sara said.

9

"The farm must be a couple of miles outside it."

"Our address is Maplewood, R.D.," Sam said precisely, "so I guess you can say we live *at* Maplewood."

He grinned down at his sister with that crooked smile of his, which was hardly more than a lift of one corner of his mouth. Sara smiled back at her twin brother. His shock of untidy hair tumbled over his forehead, as usual, and he had that absent-minded look about him, the look that came from always having something on his mind. Back home in Philadelphia all their friends called him Superbrain. But Sam didn't mind their teasing. He was good-natured and not at all stuffy about getting all A's and being able to answer the toughest questions in class.

Even though they were twins and Sara shared Sam's auburn hair and hazel eyes, their father often remarked that they were alike "in a very different way." Sara wore her hair short in a soft Princess Di wave. She was more interested in people than she was in books and had lots of friends in Philadelphia.

But although they were different in their own individual way, Sara and Sam, like most twins, shared a close relationship and had an uncanny ability to know what the other one was thinking or feeling. And right now Sara knew that Sam was as eager as she to be moving into their new home.

"Well, here we are in historic old Maplewood," Mrs. Harmon announced at last.

Sara glimpsed the historical marker by the side of the road that informed the traveler that Maplewood was an old colonial town and the site of one of the largest gristmills of the eighteenth century. The truck they had been following had turned off, and now they could see the road ahead plainly. They drove past quaint brick and stone houses, some with bright flower boxes at the windows. They rounded the

10

public square, equipped with a band shell and an old-fashioned gazebo, and drove down a street lined with small shops and businesses.

"The college is on the hill above the square," their mother said. "When we get settled, we'll have to get your father to give us a guided tour."

Looking at the tall, gray college buildings that hovered over the town, Sara's thoughts went back to the day their father had accepted the offer of chairman of the history department at Maplewood College. Dad had told them that he had always wanted to teach in a small college, where he could escape the pressures of a big university and spend more time with his students and do more research.

At first Sara and Sam weren't sure they liked the idea of leaving their home in Philadelphia. Sara would miss all her friends and the fun they had on weekends, and Sam would miss the libraries and museums that the city had to offer. But after their father had assured them that Maplewood College had a fine library and that there was a good school where there would be plenty of young people to make friends with, the twins began to look forward to their new adventure.

All that week they had helped Mom pack for the movers while their older brother, Tim, and Dad were busy painting the rooms of their new house. Now as they drove through the outskirts of Maplewood and onto the quiet country road leading to their farm, Sara said a little breathlessly, "Well, we'll soon be there!"

They passed the wooded hills and green meadows of a large horse farm where the Rabers, their nearest neighbors, lived. On the arch over the drive that led to the stable was a sign: Fox Ridge Farm, American Saddlebreds.

"Oh, look at that beautiful bay!" Sara cried.

11

Sam regarded the reddish-brown horse loping around in the corral next to the stable and whistled softly. "He sure is a beauty!"

Mrs. Harmon, negotiating a long curve in the road, called out with a happy lilt in her voice, "Only a half mile more and we'll be home!"

The twins watched eagerly for the big stone farmhouse. When they had first seen its gray limestone walls, guarded by the two big ash trees in front, they had thought the old house looked forlorn and mysterious—as if it were hiding a secret. But now as it came into view, with its bushes trimmed and its dark windows opened to the sun, they noticed how cheerful and lived-in it appeared.

As Mrs. Harmon swung into the driveway, she said, "It looks as if we have company."

Sara craned her neck in the direction of the barn, where Tim's VW jalopy was parked. A man wearing a wide-brimmed western hat was standing beside a red horse van. He was talking to their father.

When the station wagon came to a halt in front of the house, Professor Harmon left the stranger and hurried across the lawn to greet them. His long, scholarly face broke into a broad smile as he bent his tall frame over the car.

"Well, am I glad to see the rest of my family again!" he said as he opened the door and popped his head inside. He helped his wife out of the station wagon, and Sara and Sam scrambled out the other side. Tim, hearing all the commotion, yelled his greetings from a second-story window. The paintbrush in his hand was dripping blue paint.

"Before we unload the suitcases, come and meet our neighbor," their father said. "I've told you about Ed Raber, Janice, but I don't believe you've met him, and I know Sara and Sam haven't."

The man standing by the van doffed his western hat as Professor Harmon introduced his family. Ed Raber was a tall, heavy-set man with a jolly red face, sandy hair, and twinkling blue eyes that smiled down at them over a snubbed nose.

"It sure is nice to have neighbors in the old Goodwin place," he said. "Our daughter Vickie will be glad to have some young people close by. She and her mother are in Nebraska, visiting her grandmother. Too bad they can't be here to greet you."

Clamping his wide-brimmed hat on his head, he added, "Well, I'd better be going. You'll want to get settled. Just came by to see how the professor and Tim were doing."

"That was very neighborly," Mrs. Harmon said, "and we'd like to meet your family when they return."

"Oh, they'll be right anxious to meet you folks, too," Mr. Raber said with a twinkle. He turned to leave; then, as if he had just thought of something, he turned to Sara and Sam. "Do you two know how to ride?"

"Ride?" Sara asked, holding her breath.

"Yes, ride, young lady." With a chuckle he added, "I mean horses."

"Oh, yes!" Sara answered, her eyes bright. "Sam and I took riding lessons last year at a riding academy."

"Well, you're welcome to ride our trail horses any time you want to," Mr. Raber offered. "Just ask Bob Dolan—he's my trainer—to saddle them up for you, and he'll show you the trails. You see, we breed and sell American Saddlebreds, but we also run a riding stable for folks in town."

He climbed into the cab of the van and turned on the motor. With a friendly wave, he drove out of the drive and down the road in the direction of Fox Ridge Farm.

They watched until the van was out of sight around the

13

curve in the road, then Sara turned to her father with shining eyes. "Oh, Dad, can we go to Fox Ridge Farm and ride?"

Her father laughed. "I knew that would sell you on living in the country, Sara. But before you and Sam get too involved with our neighbor's horses, there are plenty of things to be done here, so stay around and give us a hand."

"Has our furniture arrived yet?" Mom asked as Dad led the way to the side door.

"It did, and Tim and I have it all placed. We painted the rooms which needed painting, too. Tim's doing the last bedroom now."

Dad opened the side door that led into an enormous kitchen. It was so large that their dining table and chairs looked right at home placed in a sunny alcove overlooking the yard. There was even an old fireplace with a brick oven alongside it and deep windowsills which already held most of Mom's plants.

While their mother explored the cabinet shelves for something for dinner, Sara and Sam started up the narrow winding staircase that led from the kitchen to the second floor. Tim came halfway down the steps to meet them.

"Hi, you two," he called. He wiped his hands on a paint cloth, then threw his arms around both of them, leaving a blue smudge on Sara's cheek. "Boy, am I glad to see you kids," he said. "I missed you. No kidding, I *really* did!"

Tim was tall, like Dad, and had dark wavy hair like Mom's. His sparkling blue eyes and broad smile were what Sara would call "infectious"—nobody could resist them, especially girls.

Even though Tim was three years older than the twins and would be a senior in high school this year, he never told them to get lost the way some older brothers did. Tim teased

14

a lot, but they could always depend on him to be there when they needed him.

Now he led the way to the upstairs hall and stopped at the first room at the top of the stairs. With an extravagant bow, he waved Sara into the room. "Your room, Mademoiselle," he said with a flourish. Tim never let them forget that he had studied French for two years.

Sara stepped into the room she had chosen to be hers when they had first inspected the old house. She had liked it because it had a bay window looking out the front and she could see up and down the road in both directions. She walked over to the bay window now and sat down in the deep window seat. Glancing around at her familiar furniture and the newly painted walls, she said, "I like the color you painted the room, Tim. A soft rose, my favorite. It's just like my bedroom at home."

"This is home now, Sara," Tim told her.

"I know," Sara muttered with a wave of homesickness for the little brick house they had left behind them in the city.

She got up and walked across the hall to Sam's room. Sam was standing by his window that overlooked the back of the house. When he heard her coming, he turned and said, "Hey, look at the neat view I get. You can even see the pond from here."

Sara gazed down at the woods that stretched from the back of their house to the large pond. In the late afternoon sun the pond looked like a golden jewel set in the velvety dark background of hemlocks.

"It's beautiful," she murmured.

"It's a marsh pond," Tim explained as he joined them by the window, "and it's full of bluegills and bass. I caught some this week, and Dad and I fried them for supper. Boy, were they good!"

15

"Does the pond belong to us?" asked Sam.

"We own this side of it," Tim replied. "Mr. Raber owns the woods on the other side."

Sara looked out at the deep woods surrounding the pond. It would be fun exploring them. Maybe there was a trail or path that led around the pond. Tomorrow she'd find out, she promised herself.

She was about to turn away from the window when something caught her eye. A thin line of smoke was rising from the tree tops directly across the pond from their house.

She turned to Tim inquiringly. "Where's that smoke coming from? Does someone live on the other side of the pond?"

Tim stepped back to the window to have a look. "No one lives there or Mr. Raber would have mentioned it. He said we were his nearest neighbors."

"It's probably just someone's campfire," Sam reasoned.

Tim shook his head. "Nobody camps over there. The campground's on the other side of Maplewood." He brought his dark brows together in a quick frown. "Better run down and tell Dad about this. I don't think Mr. Raber would want anybody making a fire in his woods. It hasn't rained for a week, and the woods are dry."

"I'll go tell Dad," Sara volunteered. "No use you dripping blue paint all over the house."

She had to run outside to find their father. He had just finished unloading the station wagon, and as she helped carry some bundles up to the house, she told him about the smoke.

Dad followed her upstairs to Sam's room. He strode over to the window, and his gray eyes scanned the woods around the pond. "Where's the smoke Sara is all excited about?" he asked.

Sam and Tim shrugged and looked puzzled.

16

"It just drifted off," Tim replied.

"There were a couple of puffs then just a thin line and now you can't see it at all," Sam added.

"Well, whoever made it must have put it out," reasoned their father. "Come down now and let's help your mother with dinner. I'm hungry enough to eat a mountain."

"So am I," Tim agreed, following Dad out of the room.

Sara came over to the window where Sam was still standing. "Well, let's go," she said.

"Okay," Sam replied.

He gave one last glance at the woods across the pond. "If there's nobody living or camping there," he wondered aloud, "then where did that smoke come from?"

He shook his head, puzzled, as he turned to follow Sara out of the room.

2

A Weird Cry

AFTER dinner they sat on the side porch and watched the night fall. The yard sparkled with fireflies, and the June night was filled with the chorus of frog sounds from the pond. Somewhere deep in the woods a screech owl called, its high wavering notes a ghostly cry.

Sara shivered as she listened. "One thing's certain," she vowed, "I'm never going into those woods at night!" Little did she know, as she sat safe and secure with her family, that only a short time later she would have to break that vow.

Her father laughed. "That owl just sounds eerie, Sara. Our woods are safer at night than city streets." He leaned back in his chair with a contented sigh. "I have always wanted to live near nature."

"And I, too," Mrs. Harmon said. "I loved growing up on our farm. We didn't have much money, but we always had enough to eat because we raised our own food." She drew a reminiscent sigh. "We canned our vegetables and fruit and made our own bread. My, how good it all tasted!"

"Are you planning for a vegetable garden here, Mom?" Sam asked. "I remember in Philly how you always said you wished we could have one."

"Indeed I am," replied Mrs. Harmon. "It will save on the food budget, and it will give us all a good workout."

Their father chuckled. "Why, we may even get a cow for our barn!"

"And some chickens, too," Sara said dreamily. "I'd just love gathering the eggs."

"Then maybe I can have two or three for breakfast instead of only one," Tim chimed in. Knowing Tim's appetite, they all laughed.

Sam changed the subject by asking, "Dad, why did Mr. Raber call our farm the old Goodwin place?"

Professor Harmon settled back to the subject he liked most, the history of things. "This farm dates back to the American Revolution," he explained. "With the help of the local historian, Pastor Reese, I found out that from the eighteenth century until just a year ago the farm had belonged to the Goodwin family. It seems that the current Goodwins couldn't make a go of it and had to sell the farm. According to Pastor Reese, they are now living in town."

"A realtor modernized the old house and put it on the market," Mom interjected. "Happily, we saw that it was for sale."

"But because the Goodwins had lived here for so long," Dad continued, "everyone got used to calling it the old Goodwin place."

"Well, now it's the Harmon place," Tim announced proudly.

"Right!" Dad agreed.

"Maybe we should give it a real name," Sara mused. "Then everyone will stop calling it the old Goodwin place."

"We have," Tim told her. "It's the Harmon place now."

"Oh, that's not a real name," Sara said, frowning. "I was thinking of something more descriptive. You know, like the Raber's Fox Ridge Farm." She wrinkled her forehead in thought, then her eyes brightened. "I know! We can call our place Marsh Pond Farm!"

"Hey, I like that," Sam said.

Tim grinned and shook his head. "I suppose you'll be giving fancy names to all the trees and flowers on the farm, Sara."

"I may," Sara said with a toss of her head. "I can't see calling things just by their common names, like Tree, Flower, or Field."

Sam laughed. "Remember, Tim, when you got that cute little puppy for your birthday and just called it Dog?"

"Hey, I'm not going to say any more," Tim said with a shake of his head. "Two against one. That's not fair." He added with a sigh, "I would have to have a sister and brother who are twins and stick together like glue."

"We're not Siamese," Sara threw back at him.

"That's enough discussion for now," Mom said, hoping to divert an argument. "Let's just relax and listen to the night sounds." She drew in a deep, satisfied breath. "It's so good to be in the country."

"Yes," Dad said, reaching for her hand, "and it's good to be all together again."

They were all tired from the excitement of moving into their new home and went to bed early that night. After he said his prayers, Sam looked out the open window to a sky studded with stars. It reminded him of a Bible verse he had learned, and he quoted softly: " 'The heavens declare the glory of God; and the firmament showeth his handiwork.' " He lay back on his pillow with a contented sigh and was soon asleep.

It seemed only a short time later that he was awakened by a strange noise. He sat up in bed and listened. The deep-throated *grr-um grr umps* and the higher *ho-wang bo-wangs* echoed through the dark night like wails from a banshee.

Sam leaped out of bed and went to the open window. He stood tense, straining his ears. The sounds, he soon discovered, came from the pond. He cocked his head thoughtfully, and then with a flash of memory, he smiled to himself. It was only the frogs in the quiet night. He closed his window to shut out the racket and slid back into bed.

When he awoke again, he discovered that he had thrown off his covers. The room was warm and stuffy. He got out of bed and threw open his window. The fresh, cool morning air swept over him as he stood looking out at the peaceful pond. All was quiet now. The frogs must be asleep. He smiled rue fully and wished they would sleep at night, like humans, and *grr-ump* together during the day.

As he glanced idly across the pond something caught his eye. It was a thin wisp of gray spiraling above the tops of the trees. The smoke again!

He closed his eyes and opened them wide, to make sure he wasn't seeing things. But the smoke was still there. Suddenly, an overwhelming desire to know what was causing it came over him, and he knew he had to find out. Right now.

He turned and glanced at his alarm clock. It was only six-thirty. He knew that Sara and the rest of the family wouldn't be up for at least another hour. That would give him time to hike around the pond to find out where the smoke was coming from. He looked back at the woods across the pond, and his eyes narrowed as he made a mental note just where he would have to go. The line of smoke was directly across from his window, so he'd have to walk only halfway around the pond to get there.

He pulled on his jeans and got into a sweatshirt. In five minutes he was quietly slipping down the back stairs to the kitchen. No use making a lot of noise and waking the rest of the family. He knew that as soon as his parents were up, there would be plenty of things Dad would want him to do.

Well, he'd do his share, but now in the quiet of the new day, he reveled at being alone on an adventure of his own. Grabbing two powdered doughnuts to tide him over until breakfast, he opened the kitchen door and stepped out onto the porch.

Taking a large bite from one of the doughnuts, he walked across the backyard, where he discovered a small path that led through the woods to an old wooden dock. When he arrived at the dock, he made another discovery. Tied alongside it was a rowboat, its paint scaling and peeling.

"Hey, neat!" he said aloud as he bent to examine the boat. It would be shorter and easier to row across the pond, but when he looked around for the oars, he couldn't find them.

Oh well, he decided, maybe the old boat leaked. He noticed that there was some water in it. What it needed was some caulking and a fresh coat of paint.

As he walked to the end of the rickety dock, its gray, sunbleached boards creaked under his feet. While he finished off the second doughnut, he looked around the pond to get his bearings. As Tim had said, it was a marsh pond all right,

Sam leaped off the dock onto a green hummock of swamp grass, disturbing a kingfisher nesting in a nearby hemlock.

with spikey reeds and cat-o'-nine-tails growing around its ragged shoreline. At one end dead tree trunks, gray and stark, rose out of the water where once the forest had been. Sam reasoned that the inlet must be at that end of the pond, and if so, the shore would be swampy. He'd walk around the pond in the opposite direction toward the outlet.

He leaped off the dock onto a green hummock of swamp grass, disturbing a kingfisher nesting in a nearby hemlock. With a sharp, grating cry the bird flapped out of the tree and flew across the pond to a tall stump sticking out of the water. Sam hopped from the hummock to a fallen tree, covered with green moss. When he found solid footing, he turned toward the outlet and walked through the woods, keeping the shoreline of the pond in view so that he'd know where he was going.

He pushed through the trees until he found what he

thought might be a deer trace. The forest floor was dark and moist, covered with leaf mold, and here and there he walked through ferns up to his knees. He paused once to marvel at the different kinds of fungi that grew on a fallen tree trunk. Stooping to examine a large one, he noticed how smooth and white it was underneath.

When he reached the outlet, he hopped across the runoff stream on logs that served as a rough kind of footbridge. He paused a moment to watch the stream disappear through the woods in a fern-covered ravine. Wow, he thought, Mom would sure like to paint this!

He turned to walk across a high weedy bank that dammed up the pond at the end of the outlet. He paused a moment on the middle of the dam bank to look across the pond to the far inlet. His eyes followed the shoreline to where he had seen the smoke just a short time ago, but he couldn't see it now. It had disappeared as suddenly as it had yesterday. However, he had a pretty good idea where it came from and continued across the dam.

The woods on the other side of the pond were overgrown with shrubs and prickly blackberry canes that tore at his clothing. When the canes thickened and blocked his way, he detoured around them through a dark grove of pines.

As he trudged through the trees, he wondered if he was opposite their house by now. The woods on this side of the pond were so thick that he had no way of telling, so he kept walking in what he thought was the right direction.

At long last he glimpsed daylight through the thick boughs ahead. Warily, he slowed his pace and kept to the shadows of the pines. The needles formed a thick, soft carpet under his feet, so that he could walk soundlessly. He moved from tree to tree until he found himself facing a small clearing.

He stood motionless and stared. There in the middle of the open space was a log cabin, and rising up from the side of it was a large stone chimney.

Sam looked at the dark windows that stared back at him like brooding eyes. Rusty pine needles had blown across a sagging, wooden porch, and several shakes were missing from the roof. From its appearance, he could see that the cabin hadn't been lived in for a long time. Yet this must have been the source of the smoke that he had observed only a short time ago, Sam mused as he glanced up at the stone chimney.

Well, he hadn't come all this way around the pond just to stand and stare at an old cabin, he told himself. He wanted some answers. Squaring his shoulders, he stuck his hands into his pockets and marched across the clearing. Boldly he stepped up on the sagging porch, carefully avoiding a broken board.

He stood for a moment, looking around the clearing, and as he did so, an eerie feeling crept over him. Everything about the clearing was silent, as if someone or something was waiting and watching.

Sam raised his fist and was about to rap on the slab-covered door, when the silence was broken by a high, shrill yowl.

E-e-e-yow!

It was a weird kind of cry—a wild, unearthly cry that sent shivers racing up and down his spine. It seemed to come from the cabin, and yet it echoed all around the clearing, completely surrounding him. It sounded so close that he was sure at any moment someone or something was going to reach out and grab him.

Leaping off the porch, Sam made a dash for the pines. He plunged through the dark trees, stumbling over fallen logs and sliding on slippery needles. He didn't look back to see if anyone or anything was following. He just kept running until he reached the pond dam where he dropped down on the weedy bank, his throat aching and his heart pounding.

Glancing across the pond to the now silent woods, he gasped aloud, "W-what-was-that?"

The eerie cry hadn't sounded like an animal or a bird. It hadn't sounded like anything he had ever heard before, yet it had to be *something*.

He looked across the pond in the direction of the cabin. If the cry hadn't come from an animal or a bird, then it had to be made by a person, even though he hadn't seen anyone around the clearing.

And that meant only one thing, he reasoned. The weird cry he had heard had to be connected with the smoke they had seen.

3

Sara's Discovery

SARA awoke only a few minutes after Sam had started his hike around the pond. She showered and dressed, but before starting down the back stairs, she knocked on her twin's door. When there was no answer, she opened the door and peeked inside the room, expecting to find Sam still sound asleep. The rumpled sheets on the bed and the pajama bottom hastily flung over a chair back told her that Sam was already up and had left in a hurry.

Sara quirked her eyebrow in a quizzical frown. Where had Sam gone off to so early in the morning and by himself?

The rest of the family was still asleep as she made her way quietly down the back stairs to the kitchen. Her eyes focused on the open box of doughnuts, and she noticed that two were missing. Sam had been here all right, but he wasn't here now.

She let herself out the back door and stood in the middle of the yard, looking around her. There had been so much to do when they arrived late yesterday afternoon that there had been no time to explore the farm. Now she glanced at the barn and down at the woods that led to the pond. She wanted to explore those woods, too, but would save that for later when she had more time.

On the other side of the house stretched a long green field. Sara decided that she'd name the field Green Meadow. And the woods she'd call Hemlock Woods because Dad had told her that most of the evergreens were hemlocks.

"Green Meadow and Hemlock Woods," she said in a sing-song voice as she started across the field in search of Sam. She smiled to herself, pleased with the way the names sounded.

She walked close to the woods that bordered the lower side of Green Meadow and discovered that now and then between the trees she could catch glimpses of the pond sparkling in the early morning sun. The field dipped down over a rise and she was out of sight of their house and barn.

At the very end of the field she found a large shed. It looked lonely tucked away in the far corner of Green Meadow with the dark hemlock woods behind it. Curiously she walked up to the door of the old building and peered through a wide crack in its weathered, gray boards. It was too dark inside to see much, so she pushed the sliding door open on its rusty rollers.

As she stepped over the threshold, she had the queer feeling that she was trespassing. But that was silly. This shed must belong to Marsh Pond Farm. It was in their field.

Sara wriggled her nose at the musty smells and peered around her. The shed was empty except for a few old gasoline cans, discarded lumber, and a rusty old hay rake. A small loft in back held several dusty bales of straw.

She walked to the back of the shed. It was dark underneath the loft, but something shiny had caught her eye. She reached up her hand and touched a horse's bridle that hung from a nail driven into the back wall.

She took the bridle down to examine it. She could see at once that it wasn't merely a bridle that had been left here along with the other old things. It looked new and expensive, like the bridles that were used on the show horses at the riding academy. The leather was soft and pliable and looked as if it had just been soaped clean. The bit, too, was still shiny as if it hadn't been used much.

Sara gazed around her. Everything else in the shed was so old and dusty that she decided someone must have left the bridle here recently. But who? Why would anyone want to leave a good bridle like this one here in this old building, she wondered.

Of course it could have belonged to the Goodwins who had lived here before them. But the Goodwin family had moved into town a year ago. Surely they would not have left an expensive new bridle here all this time.

She hung the bridle back on the peg where she had found it, and after glancing around to see if there was anything more to notice, she left the shed and pushed the sliding door shut as she had found it.

She decided to find Sam to tell him about her discovery. Maybe he'd have an explanation for why the bridle was hanging in their shed.

Where was Sam anyway?

"Sam!" she called her voice echoing along the field and

down through the woods. "Sam! Where are you?"

She paused to listen for a reply, then called out again. This time she thought she heard an answer from deep in the woods. She scrambled through the trees toward the sound of the familiar voice and found Sam coming up from the pond to meet her.

His face was flushed with excitement, and before she had a chance to tell him about her discovery in the old shed, he quickly sketched in his own events of the morning. "And after I heard that weird cry," he finished, "I ran all the way back."

He looked at the pond in the direction of the cabin and brought his brows together in a quick frown. "I feel foolish now, though. I shouldn't have run like a dumb, scared rabbit from the clearing. I should have stayed and found out what caused that crazy sound."

"Maybe it was some animal," suggested Sara. "After all, we're city kids and aren't used to strange sounds in the woods."

Sam shook his head. "It wasn't an animal."

Sara drew in a deep breath. "Well, then maybe it was an owl. They sure sound weird enough."

"It didn't sound like a bird either," Sam insisted.

Sara looked at her brother with a puzzled shake of her head. "Then what did it sound like?" She broke off and stared at Sam in astonishment. "You don't mean it sounded *human!*"

Sam nodded. "I believe the same person who made the smoke made that sound."

"But why?" asked Sara.

Sam shrugged. "I don't know, but I'm going back there to find out. And the next time I don't intend getting spooked."

Sara felt the flush of excitement on her cheeks. "I'll go

with you," she offered as they started back to the house, "and let's tell Tim about it. Maybe he'll come, too."

She let a grin pluck at her lips. "Safety in numbers, you know."

4

The Trapdoor

SARA and Sam were kept busy the rest of the morning, and it wasn't until lunchtime that Sam had the chance to tell the rest of the family about the cabin he had found on his early morning walk.

Tim looked up with interest from his cheese sandwich. "I didn't know there was a cabin over there, but then I haven't walked around the pond." His interest quickened. "Hey, maybe that's where the smoke came from that we saw yesterday."

Professor Harmon tugged thoughtfully at the lobe of his ear. "Come to think of it, I believe Ed Raber did mention that someone had once lived across the pond."

"Does anyone live there now?" Sam asked, and Sara

caught the bright excitement in his eyes.

Their father shook his head. "I don't suppose so, or Ed Raber would have mentioned it."

"But what about the smoke we saw yesterday?" Tim prompted. "From the location of where Sam said he found the cabin, it may have come from there."

"Well, maybe a hiker stopped at the cabin to spend the night and then moved on," Dad replied with a slight move of his shoulders.

When there was a lull in the conversation, Sara told about the old shed in the corner of Green Meadow. "I discovered something strange, too," she added.

"Oh-oh! Our lady sleuth is at it again," Tim broke in, a teasing glint in his eye.

Sara ignored the remark and told about the bridle she had found hanging on a nail under the loft.

"What is so mysterious about that, Sara?" Mrs. Harmon asked. "Maybe someone around here has been using the old shed as a stable to keep his horse."

Sara shook her head. "That's what's so mysterious," she returned, her eyes bright with excitement. "There's just that loft in the shed. There's no stall to keep a horse."

"Well," Dad said, scraping his chair back from the table, "I dare say whoever left an expensive new bridle there will be coming back for it."

"Yeah, that's a simple enough explanation," agreed Tim, crumpling his paper napkin and getting up from the table. "Come on, Sam, let's finish the trim in the guest room, then you can show Sara and me that cabin in the woods."

As she helped her mother remove the dishes from the table, Sara felt let down. Everyone was curious about the cabin Sam had found across the pond, but no one had taken her discovery seriously. She still believed that finding the bridle in the shed meant something. She didn't know just what, but she thought it strange than an expensive new bridle should be left hanging in an old shed that wasn't even used as a stable.

However, a half hour later her thoughts were on other things as she started out for the pond with her brothers. They took a shortcut through the woods, and when they reached the dam, Sam pointed to the shoreline across the pond where the cabin was and confided in Tim about the weird cry he had heard.

Tim, the skeptic, grinned over at his brother. "Are you sure you didn't hear some kind of animal or bird?"

"That's what I asked him," put in Sara.

Sam ran his fingers through his tousled hair. "It didn't sound like any bird or animal I know of."

"It was probably a crow," Tim said, laughing. "They make all kinds of loud, queer sounds. Sometimes they sound almost human."

"What about the smoke we saw yesterday?" Sam reminded him. "A crow didn't make that."

Tim wrinkled his nose.

"You know," Sara spoke up, "the two times the smoke was seen were late yesterday afternoon and early this morning. It could mean that someone may be making a fire to cook a meal."

"Like the hiker Dad mentioned," Tim added. He gave Sara and Sam a playful shove. "Come on, you characters, let's get going. I'd like to see that cabin."

Sam led the way across the dam bank and through the dark pine woods. When they came to the edge of the clearing, he motioned for them to stop. They stood quietly in the shadows of the trees to size up the situation.

The clearing was as silent and as deserted-looking as it

had been when Sam had seen it earlier that day. But as before, he had the eerie feeling that someone or something was waiting and watching.

Tim said softly under his breath, "Go up to the cabin and knock on the door, Sam, as you were going to do this morning. Sara and I'll hide in back of the cabin. If anyone is up to any tricks, we'll catch him."

Sam nodded and started across the clearing to the sagging porch. Tim grabbed Sara's hand and hurried her to the back of the cabin. When they reached it, they crouched down and listened to Sam's three short knocks on the slab door.

Sara's heart thumped in the long moment that passed. Then she heard Sam's rapping again, this time much louder. Tim pressed his ear against the logs of the cabin, but there was no sound from inside, and the clearing remained as silent as before.

"Wow, look what's inside!" Tim exclaimed in a hoarse whisper. "It looks like a motorcycle."

35

While they watched and listened, Sara's attention turned to the small lean-to made of unpainted boards attached to the back of the cabin. It was a flimsy affair with no door. Inside the dark lean-to something caught her eye, something bright like metal.

"Psst!" She gestured to the lean-to. "Look over there, Tim."

Silently they crept along the wall of the cabin to the lean-to.

"Wow, look what's inside!" Tim exclaimed in a hoarse whisper. "It looks like a motorcycle."

By now Sam had given up his knocking and had come around the cabin to join them. He stepped into the lean-to with Tim, and the two boys wheeled out a battered old motorcycle, repainted with silver paint. On the seat was a helmet with a visor of Plexiglas that fit down over the driver's face.

"Now we know someone's here," Sara said with satisfaction. "Someone who rides a motorcycle."

"But how did he get here?" Tim wondered, glancing around at the thick woods on all sides of the little clearing.

"Let's see if the door to the cabin is unlocked," Sara suggested. "Maybe we can find a clue inside."

The boys wheeled the motorcycle back into the lean-to and followed Sara around to the front of the cabin. "Watch the broken board," Sam warned as Sara stepped up on the porch.

They discovered that the slab door had no lock and when they pushed on it, it swung open. The three peered into the cabin.

It was empty except for a chair and table by one of the windows and a sagging cot at the other end of the one room. A battered old trunk stood at the foot of the cot.

Like stealthy intruders, they crept into the cabin and Sara walked over to the cot. She noticed at once that the blanket and pillow looked new and clean and seemed out of place with the rest of the shabby furnishings in the cabin. She bent over to examine the trunk.

It was an old-fashioned one, its rounded top bound by bands of wood fastened with bright brass nailheads. Lifting the oval top, she peered inside. The trunk contained several pairs of jeans, several men's work shirts, and a heavy leather jacket. She rooted beneath the clothes and discovered that the rest of the trunk was filled with old musty-smelling books. Wriggling her nose, she quickly shut the lid and looked around to see what her brothers had found.

Sam's lips were puckered in a soft whistle as he examined the large stone fireplace. He stooped over and gingerly touched a burned-out log. "There's been a fire here recently," he observed. "This charred wood under the ashes is still warm."

"Yeah, and look at the cans of food over here on the shelf," Tim exclaimed. "This proves that someone's living here."

"Then why didn't he answer the door when I knocked this morning?" Sam wondered. "Why that weird cry?"

Tim flicked a thoughtful look at his brother. "It frightened you away, didn't it?"

"I'll say it did!" admitted Sam.

"Well, then, that means whoever made that sound didn't want you around."

"So," Sara concluded, "whoever lives here doesn't want anyone to know it. Doesn't that make it seem all the more mysterious, Tim?"

A grin worked into the corners of his eyes. "I guess it does at that, Sara."

Sam started for the door. "I'd like to look around the clearing some more. What gets me is how the guy rides his motorcycle in and out of here."

The boys tramped out of the cabin and Sara followed. As she looked back into the room, she hesitated and frowned. Then she turned quickly and shut the door behind her.

Tim was standing in the middle of the clearing. With a puzzled shake of his head, he said, "Nobody could have gone through the woods on a motorcycle the way we came."

"Then let's look for a road or a trail of some kind on the other side of the clearing," Sam suggested.

It was Sara who first discovered the narrow weedy strip through the woods. "Hey, you guys, come over here," she called.

When Sam saw the green swatch through the trees, he exclaimed, "This must have once been an old woods road. I'll bet whoever lived here long ago used this road to get to their cabin." He was down on his hands and knees now along the edge of the clearing, examining something on the ground. Sara and Tim hovered over him as he pointed to a single tire print.

Tim stared down at the narrow print and whistled softly. "This must be the way the motorcycle gets in and out of the clearing." Now he was as excited about the mystery as the twins were. "Let's follow the road and find out where it comes out," he said eagerly.

He started out along the grassy track with Sam close on his heels. As they were about to plunge deeper into the woods, Sam looked around for Sara. When he saw her still standing by the edge of the clearing, he called out, "Aren't you coming?"

Sara glanced back at the empty cabin, then shook her head. "I guess not. I want to explore more around here."

38

Sam looked at his sister hesitantly. "Well, I hope you don't hear that weird cry."

"There doesn't seem to be anyone here now," Sara said, waving him on. "I'll be all right, and I know the way home."

Sam turned and ran to catch up with Tim. Sara watched until the big trees hid them from view, then she walked slowly back to the cabin. There was something inside that had caught her attention when they were leaving and she wanted to explore it further. She could do that herself while Sam and Tim were exploring the old road.

Sara climbed the log step to the porch and stepped across the sagging boards. The door creaked on its time-worn hinges as she pushed it open. She stepped warily inside the cabin and looked around.

Alone in the one room a strange uneasiness crept over her, and for a fleeting moment she wished that she had changed her mind and had accompanied her brothers. But when she again saw the odd indentations in the hand-hewn planks of the floor, her curiosity once more overshadowed her uneasiness.

Drawing in a deep breath, she stooped, and fitting her fingers into the finger holds, she pulled upward. With surprise she watched the floor boards open like a small door—a trapdoor!

Sara had never seen a trapdoor before, but she had read about them. Many old houses, she knew, had trapdoors leading to cellar holes where people used to store their food for the winter. Sara wondered if there was such a place underneath this trapdoor.

In her excitement to find out, she forgot her uneasiness of being alone in the cabin and swung the door all the way back. A damp, musty odor met her nostrils as she peered into the black space beneath.

When her eyes became adjusted to the dimness, she noticed what looked like a crude ladder leading downward. Slowly she started down the wooden rungs. When her foot touched the bottom, she found herself in a small underground room with stone walls and a ground floor. From the shaft of light coming through the open trapdoor, she could make out a barrel in a far corner and several old crocks and jars lined up along the walls.

She took several steps forward then leaped back, startled, as something sticky and repulsive brushed her face. She reached up hastily to brush it away, and discovered that it was an enormous cobweb.

Ugh, she muttered, making her way quickly through the web. She hoped there weren't any bats or mice down here. Spiders were enough!

She was bending over to examine the contents of a barrel in the far corner when she thought she heard a creak on the cabin floor above. She straightened up and listened, her heart pounding like a jackhammer.

There it was again. Was there someone up there? But how could there be, she thought. She had been alone in the cabin.

Then she remembered that she had forgotten to shut the cabin door behind her. Anyone could have entered the cabin and she wouldn't have noticed down here in the cellar hole.

Above the pounding of her heart, she listened intently, but now all seemed quiet in the cabin room. My imagination again, she scolded herself. But it sure is scary down here. One quick look in the barrel and I'm getting out.

She bent over the barrel again, and at that moment she heard a loud scraping sound above her. This time she knew she wasn't imagining the footfalls on the cabin floor. She straightened up and hurried toward the ladder. But it was too late. The trapdoor slammed shut above her, and she was left in total darkness.

She groped her way to the ladder and stumbled up it until she could reach the trapdoor. She pushed against it, but it wouldn't lift upward. With all her strength she pushed, but the trapdoor wouldn't budge. She yelled and pounded on it, but nobody answered.

Her throat husky and her knuckles raw, she held her breath, listening. No longer did she hear the scraping sound nor the footsteps on the floor above. There was only a deadly silence now, and she knew that she was alone again in the cabin.

Alone and trapped in the cellar hole.

5

Fox Ridge Farm

SAM and Tim followed the old woods road until it came out to a large field. They climbed under a barbed-wire fence and walked to the top of the field to look around. Tim gestured toward the buildings on the far side.

"Fox Ridge Farm," he said.

Sam squinted at the large stable, the barn, and the white farmhouse beyond. "Do you think Mr. Raber knows about the motorcycle we found at the cabin?" he asked. "After all, it's on his property."

"Could be," Tim said. "Let's find out."

They cut across the field and walked past the barn to the stable. In the corral they saw a man of slight build who appeared to be in his thirties, with curly blond hair. He was exercising a beautiful buckskin mare. When he saw the boys, the man waved a friendly greeting and rode over to the corral fence.

"What can I do for you?" he asked. "Do you want to ride?"

"Not really," Tim answered. "I'm Tim Harmon and this is my brother Sam. We just moved into the farm by the marsh pond."

"Oh, the old Goodwin place," the man said. He hesitated a moment, his sharp blue eyes looking them over. Then he leaned over in the saddle and thrust out his hand "My name's Bob Dolan. I'm Mr. Raber's trainer. Since we're neighbors, I might as well show you around."

He seemed very obliging as he got down from his mount and opened the corral gate for them. He led the way into the stable, equipped with a tack room in the front and a long aisle beyond, stalls on either side. As they walked along the stalls, Sam noticed two newborn colts lying in the straw next to their mothers.

"We got some of the best breeding mares in the county," Bob explained, "and they have gentle dispositions and are safe enough for any dude to ride." He paused and smiled down at the colts. "In a day or two they go out to pasture. Cute little fellas, aren't they?"

"They sure are," Sam said, wishing Sara were here to see the colts.

They moved on through the stable and stopped before the stall of a beautiful chestnut-brown stallion. "Beauty, here, is our prize stallion. He's an American Saddlebred," Bob said proudly. "Mr. Raber takes him to all the horse shows. We had a white American Saddlebred, too, that we used to show. Beauty and White Lightning's ribbons are all over the wall of the tack room."

"You said 'used to show,' " Sam broke in. "Did Mr. Raber sell White Lightning?"

Bob Dolan's friendly smile quickly changed into a frown, and Sam noticed the muscles about his mouth tightening. "No, he didn't sell the stallion. Somehow White Lightning got out of his stall, and we never saw him again. Mr. Raber thinks someone let him out and then took him off in a horse van."

"You mean stole him?" Tim asked with surprise.

Bob nodded and turned away.

"Why does he think that?" Sam persisted.

"Because I always make sure the bolts on the stalls are fastened and the corral gate is securely closed every day before I quit work. Now, ever since the night White Lightning disappeared, we've put a lock on the corral gate, and I've been sleeping on a cot in the tack room."

"I guess if White Lightning was an American Saddlebred, he was worth a lot of money," Tim suggested.

Bob nodded. "He sure was."

"Doesn't Mr. Raber have any idea who stole White Lightning?" Sam asked.

Bob twitched his shoulders. "He still hasn't traced the stallion, even though he notified all the stables and horse dealers around. He thinks it's the work of a gang of horse thieves because a couple of other stables near here have reported missing thoroughbreds, too."

"Wow, horse rustlers here in Pennsylvania!" Tim exclaimed. He shook his head in disbelief. "I thought they were only out West."

They continued walking past the stalls. "Does Mr. Raber have any other American Saddlebred stallions besides Beauty?" asked Sam.

The smile returned to Bob's face. "I reckon we'll have

another one any minute now. I'm waiting for Mr. Raber to come with the van. He went to the Lancaster horse auction today to pick one up. Hang around and you'll get to see it."

Sam and Tim had been so interested in what Bob was telling them about the missing Saddlebred that they had almost forgotten what they had come here for in the first place. In a brief pause in the conversation, Sam cleared his throat and asked, "Bob, does anyone live in that old cabin in the woods by the pond?"

Bob Dolan shook his head. "Folks around here say that cabin's been empty ever since old Henry Taylor died. Henry built it himself. He was a kind of hermit and just kept to himself back there, reading his books all day. He died shortly before Mr. Raber bought Fox Ridge Farm, but Mr. Raber never bothered to tear down the cabin. Said it wasn't in anyone's way back there in the woods."

"We saw a motorcycle parked in back of the cabin today," Tim informed Bob.

The horse trainer looked surprised. "You did?"

Both boys nodded. Then Bob went on, "Well, I reckon it must belong to a kid from town. Kids ride dirt bikes all around here."

"This one didn't look much like a dirt bike," Sam explained. "It looked more like an old, silver-painted motorcycle."

Bob raised a quizzical eyebrow, then his blue eyes sharpened. "Sounds like Huy Chau's cycle. Huy's a Vietnamese refugee who lives in Maplewood. Came here looking for work, and Mr. Raber hired him. Rides to work on an old motorcycle just like the one you described."

Bob broke off and looked thoughtful for a moment. "Today's Huy's day off," he said. "I'll bet he's out on that cycle exploring the countryside."

45

"You say he lives in town?" Tim inquired.

Bob nodded. "That's what he told Mr. Raber and me. I guess that's why he bought that old motorcycle, to ride back and forth—" Bob's voice trailed off as a sudden rumbling sound came from the drive leading up to the stable. They turned to see a cloud of dust rising up from the lane as the red van rolled up to the corral.

"Here comes Mr. Raber now with the Saddlebred," Bob said. "Sorry I can't talk any longer, fellas, but I got to help get that new stallion into the corral and settled."

He hurried across the corral to open the gate so that Mr. Raber could drive the van through it. After Bob shut the gate, Mr. Raber got out of the cab and waved a greeting at Sam and Tim.

He looked dapper today in a tan sport jacket and his western hat. In the breast pocket of his jacket Sam noticed a neatly folded handkerchief with gaudy red and black squares on it. Sam grinned. Mr. Raber sure goes in for flashy handkerchiefs, he thought.

Bob opened the back of the van and carefully led a handsome black stallion down the ramp to the corral. The American Saddlebred was a proud, high-stepping horse. His neck arched gracefully, and his head was held high. His pointed ears were alert to his new surroundings. He carried his tail high, and his skin was all black and shone like satin.

"What a beauty!" Sam murmured under his breath, again wishing that Sara could be here to see the new stallion.

The boys stepped back as the big horse balked, then reared up on his hind legs. Bob grabbed the lead rope and started to talk softly to the Saddlebred. Soon the black stallion settled down and allowed Bob to lead him to his stall in the stable. Sam watched breathlessly, admiring the skill with which the trainer handled the spirited stallion.

"Come on," Mr. Raber said, motioning the boys to follow. "Now you can get a closer look at Black Cloud."

By the time they reached Black Cloud's stall, Bob had the door closed and the latch fastened securely. The big stallion was already nosing his oats.

"What a beauty!" Sam said again.

"He'll make a good show horse once we get him trained," Mr. Raber said proudly. "That's Bob's job. He has a way with Saddlebreds and is the best trainer around."

A look of pride brightened Bob's face as he patted Black Cloud on the rump.

After admiring the stallion a few minutes longer, they followed Mr. Raber out of the stable.

"I guess we better get going," Tim said.

"Yeah," Sam agreed.

"Well, you're welcome to come by any time to see Black Cloud," Mr. Raber invited. "Bring your sister with you the next time."

"Thanks," Sam said. "She's really nuts about horses."

Mr. Raber laughed. "I know what you mean, having a daughter of my own. Maybe you and Sara would like to ride our trail horses. They can always use the exercise."

"She'd love that," Sam said, "and so would I."

They left the corral and started down the lane. "Mr. Raber and Bob Dolan sure are neat neighbors," Sam remarked.

Tim nodded. "They sure are. Too bad that Saddlebred is missing."

"Yeah," Sam agreed with a sigh, "but at least we know who owns that silver motorcycle parked by the cabin." He paused thoughtfully. "I wonder if Huy was the creep who scared me away from the cabin with that weirdo cry."

"Yeah," Tim added. "I wonder why he'd want to do that.

Maybe he wanted to camp out at the cabin and didn't want anyone around."

"Could be," Sam agreed with a shrug.

By now they had come to the road. Sam stopped short. "Hey, Tim, aren't we going back to the cabin for Sara?"

"She'll be home by now," Tim answered. "Come on. The road's shorter than going through the woods and all the way around the pond."

Sam was about to follow Tim, but just then he had a funny feeling about his twin. It was that uncanny feeling they often had about each other. And right now Sam had the feeling that he should go back to the pond for Sara.

"I'm going back to the cabin," he pronounced as he climbed under the fence and started across the field. "Sara might be there waiting for us."

"You're sure you know the way from here?" Tim called back.

"Of course," Sam said indignantly. "After all, who was it who found the motorcycle track through the woods in the first place?" He was getting tired of Tim always treating him like a baby brother. He and Sara were fourteen and old enough to take care of themselves.

"Okay-okay," Tim said, "but I'm taking the road home. I've done enough tramping through the woods for one day. Besides, Dad may need me for something."

The boys parted, Tim whistling his way up the road and Sam cutting across the field toward the woods. Sam didn't know why he was jogging instead of walking, but for some strange reason he thought he should get back to that cabin as quickly as possible.

6

Sam to the Rescue

SARA shivered as she huddled miserably in a damp corner of the cellar hole. It was no use to keep yelling for help and pounding on the trapdoor. No one could hear her now. There were no sounds of footsteps on the floor above; the cabin was quiet. Besides, her throat ached and her knuckles were bruised.

She tried to shut out the anxious thoughts that kept whirling about in her head. Who had shut the trapdoor so that she couldn't get out? Why would anyone want to keep her in this dark cellar hole?

She thought again about the footsteps she had heard crossing the cabin floor. Someone must have deliberately wanted to shut her into the cellar. Surely her yelling and pounding could have been heard in the cabin above. She wondered if the footsteps belonged to the same person who had built the fire in the fireplace and had frightened Sam away with that weird cry.

Where were Sam and Tim now, she wondered. Maybe they were miles away by now. What if they returned home by another way and didn't come back to the cabin? She began to worry. How long would she have to remain here in the cold and the dark?

Asking herself these questions, Sara began to feel panicky. Then she remembered what Dad always said. "When you are in trouble, ask God to help. With God on your side, the trouble won't seem so bad."

Sara hugged her knees against the chill of the cellar hole and closed her eyes. "Please, God, lead Sam or Tim back to this cabin so that I can be found."

A familiar Bible verse came to her mind just then and saying it aloud made her feel braver. " 'Though I walk through the valley of the shadow of death, I will fear no evil, for thou art with me.' "

Knowing that God cared and that he was here with her made Sara feel much better, and she sat back against the stone wall of the cellar hole somewhat calmer.

o   o   o

Sam jogged all the way across the field and through the woods. When he came to the clearing he slumped down on a log to catch his breath. While he rested, he studied the clearing. As before, it was silent and empty.

He called Sara's name, but only his own echo answered him. He stared intently at the cabin. If Sara was in there, she would have heard him calling by now and would have come out.

50

She must have gone home, he told himself. Tim was right. They had been gone a long time, and she probably got tired of waiting for them.

He got up from the log and walked across the clearing. He was about to enter the pine woods when, impulsively, he stopped to glance back at the cabin. Maybe he had better check inside anyway, he decided. Sara may have left a note telling them where she had gone. She often did that.

He climbed up on the rickety porch and pushed open the slab door. Holding on to the edge of the opened door, he peered in at the empty cabin room. He didn't see a note on the table, where Sara most likely would have left one, but he did notice that something inside the cabin was different. Then his eyes fixed on the old chest that was sitting in the middle of the cabin floor.

It hadn't been there before, he told himself. It had been at the foot of the cot when they were exploring the cabin. Could Sara have moved it there for some reason, he wondered.

Curiously he walked up to the trunk and flung open the lid. He was surprised to find it half-filled with books. Probably old Henry Taylor's books. Sam was about to pick one up and riffle through its musty pages when he heard a faint cry.

He dropped the book and looked all around him. He was sure he was alone in the cabin. He ran to the open door and glanced outside, but the clearing was empty.

The cry sounded again, and now Sam was sure it came from right here in the cabin. "But where?" he asked aloud, his eyes probing into the shadowy corners. There was no one in this cabin but himself.

"Where are you?" he called back as loudly as he could. This time he made out the muffled words: "Down here!"

He stared incredulously at the old trunk. The voice seemed to be coming from there. No—*underneath* the trunk.

He pushed at the trunk. It was heavy with all those books in it. He drew in a deep breath and pushed again.

Why didn't it move? he wondered. Then he saw that the edge of it was stuck in a crack in the floor boards. He walked to the other end of the trunk and by lifting up and pulling at the same time, he managed to move it over the crack. With a loud scraping sound the trunk slid across the floor. Sam looked down where it had stood, and then he saw the trapdoor. The muffled cry sounded again on the other side of it.

He got down on his hands and knees and put his mouth close to the crack in the floor. "Sara, are you down there?"

Sara was a sight. Sam would have laughed if she hadn't looked so frightened. Like a bewildered owl she blinked her eyes in the light.

"Yes," came the hoarse reply. "Lift up the trapdoor. Get me out!"

Sam found the finger holds and pulled upward. The trapdoor opened, and Sara's frightened face peered up at him.

She was a sight, and he would have laughed if she hadn't looked so frightened. Her hair was covered with dusty gray cobwebs, and dark smudges were streaked across her face. Like a bewildered owl she blinked her eyes in the light, then she grinned a wide grin.

"Sam! Am I glad to see you. How did you get the trapdoor open?"

"I moved that," Sam said, pointing to the heavy trunk. "It was sitting right on top of the trapdoor. No wonder you couldn't get out. What happened? How did you get down there in the first place?"

Sara climbed out of the cellar hole and shivered. "It's a long story," she said through chattering teeth. "Let's go out and sit in the sun. I've never felt so cold and clammy in my whole life."

"Okay, but first I want to see what's down here," Sam said, starting down the ladder.

"There's nothing but an old cellar hole," Sara called after him, "and I'm staying up here. I never want to go down there again!"

After a few minutes exploring, Sam climbed up the ladder and shut the trapdoor. They left the cabin and sat on a log in the clearing.

"Oh my, the sun feels good," Sara said hoarsely, running her hands up and down her bare arms.

"Here, let me brush the cobwebs out of your hair, and take this handkerchief to wipe the smudges off your face." Sam reached into his pocket and handed her a clean folded handkerchief. While he picked the cobwebs out of her hair, she rubbed furiously at the smudges.

"Now tell me all about it," Sam said eagerly. "How in the world did you get into the cellar hole with that heavy trunk on top of the trapdoor? You're not a magician, you know."

Sara told about finding the trapdoor and exploring the old cellar hole. She told about the footsteps she had heard in the cabin and the loud scraping sound on the cabin floor.

"That must have been when the trunk was pushed across the floor to the trapdoor so you couldn't get out," Sam explained. "Did you see who did it?"

Sara shook her head. "By the time I stumbled up to the ladder in the dark the trapdoor was shut, and I couldn't open it."

"Do you have *any* idea who did it?" Sam persisted. "You know, by the sound of his footsteps or anything he said?"

Sara looked angry. "He didn't say anything and I have no idea who it was by the sound of his footsteps. I just had the feeling that it was someone who wanted to keep me down there for some dumb reason."

"Hmm." Sam stood up and plunged his hands into the back pockets of his jeans. "There sure is something funny going on around here."

"You can say that again!"

Sam walked over to the lean-to. "You didn't hear anyone coming or leaving the clearing?" he asked.

"How could I?" replied Sara. "I couldn't hear much of anything down in that dark hole. All I heard were those footsteps and that scraping sound across the floor."

Sam peered into the lean-to. "The motorcycle's gone," he announced. "You didn't hear anyone riding away?"

Sara shook her head.

"That's funny," Sam reflected, raking his fingers through

his tousled hair. "Motorcycles make a lot of noise. The guy must have wheeled it out of the clearing."

Suddenly he swung around and stared at his sister. "Of course!" he cried, striking his hand against his forehead. "Why didn't I think of that before? Huy Chau!"

"Huy who?" asked Sara, grinning at the way it sounded, despite her anger.

"The Vietnamese refugee who works for Mr. Raber," Sam replied. Then he told Sara how he and Tim had followed the woods road to Fox Ridge Farm where they met Bob Dolan, Mr. Raber's horse trainer. "Bob told Tim and me that Huy comes to work riding an old silver-painted motorcycle."

"Why do you think this Huy character shut me in the cellar hole?" asked Sara.

"He's our only suspect," Sam replied. "His motorcycle's gone, and that means he must have been here at the cabin when you were exploring the cellar hole."

"But why would he want to keep me down there?" Sara asked, her anger returning.

Sam could only answer with a puzzled shake of his head. "I don't know. Maybe for the same dumb reason he scared me away from the cabin this morning."

On the way back through the pines they talked more about the possibilities of Huy Chau being the culprit. Then Sam told Sara about Mr. Raber's Saddlebreds and about the missing stallion.

"Mr. Raber thinks a gang of horse thieves stole White Lightning," he said.

"How awful!" Sara exclaimed. "I hope nothing happens to his other two Saddlebreds. I can't wait to see them. Let's go to Fox Ridge Farm tomorrow."

Sam nodded agreement. He was as anxious as Sara to go

to Fox Ridge Farm, but not only to see the Saddlebreds again. If he went back there tomorrow, he'd be able to meet Mr. Raber's hired hand, and he had a lot of questions to ask this mysterious Huy Chau.

7

Huy Chau

COMING from the woods, they saw Tim swinging in a hammock he had put up between two trees in the yard. When their brother saw them, he called out, "Well, I see you found her, Sam. What were you doing at the cabin all this time, Sara?" Not waiting for an answer, he added, "Did you find any clues we overlooked?"

"I found a trapdoor that leads into a cellar hole," Sara replied. She would have told Tim about her adventure in the cabin, but at that moment their mother stepped out on the side porch to announce dinner.

Sara fled to the bathroom to wash her hands and face and to comb her hair. She slid into her place at the table just as her father was coming into the kitchen.

After Professor Harmon said grace and they started to eat, Sam and Tim told their parents about their visit to Fox Ridge Farm.

"Dad," said Sam, "do you know a Huy Chau, who is a Vietnamese refugee in Maplewood? He works for Mr. Raber."

Professor Harmon frowned thoughtfully. "I know a Dzung Chau. A man in our history department, Jim Burton, has a foster son by that name. He didn't mention a Huy, though. Of course Chau is a common Vietnamese surname. Huy may be sponsored by another family."

Tim changed the subject by asking his parents, "Do you know that Mr. Raber had one of his American Saddlebreds stolen?"

Professor Harmon nodded. "Yes, he told me. He seemed terribly upset about it."

They fell into silence for a moment. Sara hoped that Sam wouldn't say anything about finding her in the cellar hole of the cabin. If Mom and Dad knew that someone had intentionally shut her in there, they might not let them go back to the cabin again. She glanced quickly across the table at her twin.

Sam grinned impishly back at her and mouthed the words, "I won't tell!" In the next breath he turned to his parents and said, "Mr. Raber said that Sara and I could exercise his trail horses." He paused then added, "We'd really be doing him a favor."

Sara's face shone with a happy glow. "Oh, Mom, could we?"

Mrs. Harmon laughed. "I don't think we can stop you, Sara, when it comes to horses." She looked over at her husband. "If it's all right with your father, it's all right with me."

"As long as you get your chores done first," Dad reminded them. "Remember, we just moved here and there's still a lot of work to be done."

"Yeah, and Mom has to have time for her artwork," Tim added, "so we all have to help her."

"I know!" Sara gave her older brother a meaningful look. Turning to her mother, she said, "That reminds me, Mom, I found a perfect studio for you. It's that big shed across the field where I found the bridle. You can't see it from the house because it's sort of nestled down in the corner of the woods."

Professor Harmon looked up and nodded. "That would make a good studio, Jan. After we get our work done here at the house and barn, the boys and I will start remodeling that shed."

Mrs. Harmon's face beamed as she looked around at each member of her family. "Oh, how sweet of you all, I've always wanted a studio of my own—a place to spread out my canvases."

"We'll even throw in a skylight for you, Mom," Sam said generously.

o   o   o

The twins hurried through their chores the next morning, then started out for Fox Ridge Farm. They pedaled down the road on their bikes and in no time they were there.

They found Bob Dolan in the stable, mucking out the stalls. He was singing off key as he worked but broke off when he saw them. Leaning on his broom handle, he gave Sara a friendly nod as Sam introduced her.

"Sara really rides better than I," Sam added generously.

"That so?" Bob said, grinning. "Well, we'll see about that."

While he went to the tack room for saddles and bridles, Sam showed Sara Beauty and Black Cloud. Sara walked on past the stalls and looked at the mares and the little colts. "Oh, aren't they darling!" she exclaimed as she leaned over their stall doors and watched the colts.

When Bob came back with the tack, he chose two trail horses for them to ride.

"This one's named Dusty," he said, throwing the saddle over a gentle gray mare. "I think you may like to ride her, Sara."

He opened the stall door next to Dusty's and led out a brown mare with a white mark between her eyes. "And this is your horse, Sam. Her name is Blaze."

They helped Bob tack up. When the two horses were bridled and saddled, Bob led them to the corral. "Ride around several times so I can be sure you can handle them okay."

The twins mounted, and Bob watched as they walked their horses around the corral. When they reached the far end of the corral, Sara leaned over in her saddle and with a twinkle in her eye said, "Let's put our mounts through their gaits, Sam. That'll prove to Bob that we can ride."

"Right on!" Sam said, grinning. "Here goes."

With a nudge of encouragement to their horses, they jogged and loped. Clamping their knees against their mounts' withers and relaxing the reins, they went into a gallop.

Sara rode easily, as if she were a part of her mount. The wind rushed against her cheeks and a thrill of joy raced through her, as it always did when she was in the saddle. She brought Dusty to an easy loping stride again, and the gray mare moved like a dream, the muscles beneath her shiny coat moving in easy rhythm with her long graceful legs. Sara felt that she could ride the mare forever.

At last they slowed the horses to a walk and reined in by

the stable door. They knew just by looking at Bob that he was surprised at what he saw.

"Hey, you kids ride okay for me!" he praised. "A whole lot better than most of the dudes that come here for trail rides. As soon as I get the stalls done, I'll saddle up and show you the trails."

Sara was about to offer to help with the stalls so that they could get started sooner, but Sam spoke up just then. "Is Huy Chau here today? I don't see his motorcycle."

Bob pointed across the field. "He's mending fence over there. He keeps his motorcycle in back of the barn when he's here."

"Can we ride over and say hello while you finish the stalls?" Sam asked.

Bob nodded and opened the corral gate for them.

On the far side of the field they found a tall, slim boy about Tim's age. He was busy stretching a strand of barbed wire from one fence post to another with a fence stretcher.

Sam dismounted to help the boy hold the wire taut while he nailed a staple into the post. The boy nodded his thanks but didn't say anything.

"I'm Sam Harmon and this is my sister, Sara," Sam ventured. "We just moved into the old Goodwin place down the road."

Without offering his own name or saying a word, the Vietnamese boy looked up briefly and reached out to take the fence stretcher from Sam.

"Are you Huy Chau?" Sam asked.

The boy half-nodded and went on stretching the next strand of wire.

He isn't very sociable, Sara thought as she watched Huy go about his work as if they weren't there.

Sam must have realized this, too, because he came right

to the point. "Say, Huy, was that your motorcycle we saw yesterday in the lean-to behind the cabin by the pond?"

Huy turned with a sullen look. He didn't even answer Sam.

Sara felt herself getting impatient with this unfriendly boy. She dismounted, and walking up to where he was standing, she looked him straight in the eye. "Did you shut the trapdoor on me when I was in the cellar hole?" she accused. "And did you push the heavy trunk over it so that I couldn't get out?"

The Vietnamese boy shrugged as though he didn't know what she was talking about and turned his back on them.

Sam strode over to his horse and started to mount. With a slight edge to his voice he said, "I think Mr. Raber might like to know that someone with a silver-painted motorcycle is staying in his cabin."

At that Huy dropped the fence stretcher and swung around to face them. His sullen face now showed fear and his dark eyes looked desperate. To their surprise he blurted out in a frightened voice. "You not tell Mr. Raber!"

Sara's face flushed indignantly. "Why shouldn't we? Especially since you shut that trapdoor on me!"

"I would let you out," Huy Chau said, "but you not there when I get back."

"You'd better start from the beginning, Huy," Sam said in a sober voice. "I'm all mixed up."

"So am I," Sara said, flouncing down in the grass by the fence. She was still angry at the stubborn boy. "You better level with us, Huy, and now!" she threatened.

Sam joined them by the fence, and with a sigh of resignation, Huy told his story.

"I and Little Brother come to America. Church in Philadelphia sponsor us. Little Brother taken to foster home here. We not wanting to be separated. We wanting to live like brothers."

"Is your little brother's name Dzung?" Sam broke in, remembering what his father had said about Jim Burton's foster son.

Huy nodded. "You know?" he asked eagerly.

"Our dad knows his foster family," Sam replied. "I'm sure he has a good home."

Huy nodded soberly. "Good family—yes. But Little Brother's foster family not wanting two Vietnamese boys. Wanting only Dzung. I promise old grandmother before we leave Vietnam that we stay together like brothers."

"Were you sent to a foster family, too?" Sara asked, her anger for this sullen boy quickly ebbing away. She'd never want to be separated from her brothers either.

Huy shook his head. "I stay in Philadelphia with other Vietnamese who are having no foster homes. I get job in city this summer. Save money to buy secondhand motorcycle. I find out in church office where Dzung is. I quit job and come here."

"And you've been living in the cabin by the pond ever since then," Sam concluded.

Huy nodded. "Dzung hear about cabin from friends he make in Maplewood. He tell me to hide there. Bring pillow and blanket from foster parents' house. Bring food and pan to cook in." Huy paused with a wry grin. "Dzung learn to steal good in Vietnam. He is street-beggar once."

"Oh!" Sara drew in a quick breath, shocked and dismayed that Huy's little brother had had to steal and beg for his food.

There was a tightening in Sam's voice, too, as he asked, "When I came to the cabin yesterday morning, you didn't want me to know that you were living there, did you, Huy?

So you made that weird sound to frighten me away. How did you do it?"

Huy smiled. "Is old Vietnamese trick. I shout into empty juice can and it sound like so."

Sam grinned. "Well, it sure frightened me off all right." He sobered. "But why did you shut Sara in the cellar?"

Huy stole a glance at Sara and shifted uneasily on the grass. "I do not mean harm. When you discover I live in cabin, I want to hide motorcycle and clothes in cave I find in woods; so while I do this, I keep Sara in cellar so she cannot see me and follow. But when I come back to let her out, she gone."

"Sam returned to the cabin and found me," Sara explained stiffly. "And I certainly was glad to get out of that damp, dark cellar hole."

Huy lowered his eyes. "Am sorry, Sara." Then slumping against the fence post, he looked at them pleadingly. "If you tell Mr. Raber, he will send me back to Philadelphia, and I can not be with Little Brother."

"Oh, we wouldn't want that!" Sara exclaimed. She looked at Sam, and when their eyes met, she knew he was thinking the same thing.

"Look, Huy," she said, "why don't you come home with us. We have plenty of room in our house, and I know Dad and Mom will figure something out so that you and Dzung can be together."

Huy looked frightened. "No! No! Not want to make trouble, please."

"But . . ." Sara protested.

"Wait a minute," Sam broke in. "I think I understand how Huy feels, Sara. He can't trust strangers yet, especially grown-ups. I think it's better if he stays at the cabin until we can think of some way to help him. We're the only ones who

64

know he's there, except Dzung."

"And Tim," added Sara. "He was with us when we found Huy's motorcycle."

"We'll have to explain to Tim," Sam said, "but I know he won't say anything. He'll want to do everything he can to help."

The Vietnamese boy looked anxiously at Sam and then at Sara. "You and big brother not tell?"

"We'll keep your secret until we can find a way to help you and Dzung stay together," Sara promised.

Huy flashed them a broad smile. "You are okay kids."

Sam glanced at his watch. "We better get back to the corral. Bob will probably be finished mucking out the stalls by now."

Huy whistled through his teeth, and Dusky and Blaze, who had been grazing nearby, turned their heads at the boy's call.

While they waited for the horses, Sara looked at the Vietnamese boy intently. And then she said, "When Sam and I have a problem, we always pray about it. God is your friend, too, Huy. He will help you find a way to be with Dzung."

Huy looked down at his work shoes and shook his head. "I no know your God."

"Well, then I'll pray for you," Sara said earnestly.

Sam gave the boy a tilted grin. "With God and Sara on your side, Huy, you can't lose!"

Huy held the horses while the twins mounted. He waved good-bye as they started back across the field.

As she nosed Dusty close to Blaze, Sara said, "Well, Huy cleared up one mystery for us."

"*One* mystery?" asked Sam, giving his sister a quizzical look.

"Yes, now we know who's staying in the cabin across the pond."

"Is there another mystery?" Sam wanted to know.

With a puzzled shake of her head Sara said, "Well, I'd still like to know how that bridle got into our shed."

Sam laughed. "I don't know why you keep worrying about someone leaving a bridle in the shed, Sara."

"Neither do I, really," Sara admitted, sitting forward in her saddle, her sandy eyebrows drawn into a frowning line. "But you know, Sam, I just can't help the funny feeling I have about that bridle. It doesn't make sense why anyone would leave an expensive bridle like that one in our old shed and then just forget about it."

8

A Sound in the Night

BOB Dolan's horse was saddled, and he was waiting for them when they reached the stable.

"Let's get going," he said, leading the way out of the corral. He took them over the beginner's trail first, an easy track in the open, circling across the fields around the farm. But it was the trail which wound up the wooded ridge in back of the farm that thrilled Sara.

The trail climbed through shadowy rhododendron glens and past rocky ledges. Near the steep upper half of the ridge it became a switchback that came out to a wooded grove of beech trees at the top.

Bob led them to a ledge of rocks where they dismounted and tied their horses. Sara and Sam followed him on foot to the top of the ledge where they could see the entire countryside above the treetops.

"See, there's the college chapel steeple," Bob said, pointing to the hazy spire that rose above the other buildings in Maplewood.

"That's where our father works," Sara said. "I wonder if we can see the history.building from here."

"This is a neat ridge," Sam added. "I can see now why Mr. Raber called his farm Fox Ridge. Are there really foxes around here?"

Bob squatted down and picked up a stone which he rolled around in his hand. "Mr. Raber told me the farm was named Fox Ridge because in the old days there was a lot of fox hunting on this ridge. In fact the ledge we're standing on has a fox den in it. I'll show you when we get down."

· "You sure know a lot about this country, Bob," Sara said. "Did you live around here all your life?"

Bob shook his head. "No, I came from out of state. I been here only three years."

"Well, you learned a lot about horses in those three years," Sara remarked with admiration.

Bob gave a little laugh. "Oh, I've always been working at stables. Mr. Raber wouldn't have hired me if I hadn't been experienced with horses."

Sara was about to ask at what other stables he had worked, but Bob quickly changed the subject by looking at his watch and saying, "We best be going. I got a heap of work to do back at the stable."

They climbed down from the ledge, but before they left Fox Ridge, Bob showed them the fox den. He pointed out a large crevice in the rock that led back to a cave-like den. When the twins peered into the crevice, it was so dark they couldn't see a thing, but the fresh droppings at the opening

"There's the college chapel steeple," Bob said, pointing to the hazy spire that rose above the other buildings in Maplewood.

told them that an animal lived there.

"I hope nobody hunts this fox," retorted Sara.

"Don't fret, little lady," Bob assured her. "Mr. Raber doesn't allow hunting on his property. Not with all the horses around."

The ride down the ridge was as pleasant as the ride up. Dusty and Blaze were surefooted and alert and took the trail with ease. Now and then Sara reached over to pat Dusty's neck. The gentle gray mare tossed her head up and down as if acknowledging her rider's assurance.

When they reached the stable, Bob spoke the words Sara had been hoping for. "You two can ride anytime you like. You're good riders, and Dusty and Blaze need the exercise.

Just be sure to saddle and bridle up properly and rub down your horses after you've ridden them. If you've ridden them hard, walk them around the corral a couple of times to cool them off before rubbing them down. The rub rags, brushes, and currycombs are in the tack room."

"You mean we can groom our own horses?" squealed Sara with delight. "At the riding academy only the grooms were allowed to do that."

"If you ride here, you take care of your horses," Bob said. He paused with a grin. "Of course, paying patrons get that done as part of the fee."

"Well, since we're not paying patrons, we'd better get busy," Sam said, flashing Sara his crooked grin.

They put Dusty and Blaze in their stalls, then followed Bob to the tack room which was filled with saddles, bridles, and other riding equipment. Sara noticed that several of the bridles that hung from pegs on the wall were similar to the bridle she had found in their old shed. She nudged Sam and gestured to the bridles, but Sam was more interested in a large trunk with Fox Ridge Farm painted on its lid in big red letters. Beneath the lettering was the picture of a fox head.

"What's the trunk for?" he asked curiously.

"That's the trunk Mr. Raber takes to horse shows," Bob answered. "It holds tack and all his gear for the shows."

The twins glanced around the room. As Bob had said, the walls were covered with ribbons that White Lightning and Beauty had won. The ribbons and Bob's cot, along the far wall, reminded Sara of the missing stallion.

Bob nodded to the rack where they could put their saddles, then handed them each a rug rag, brush, and currycomb. Sara soon discovered that it was almost as much fun grooming Dusty as it was riding her. She rubbed down Dusty's coat, then brushed the mare's flanks and combed the tangled mane and tail with the currycomb. Dusty nickered contentedly and dropped her head to nuzzle Sara, as if to tell the girl how good it all felt.

When Sara finished grooming Dusty, she went into Blaze's stall to see how Sam was doing.

Poor Sam! He stood with rub rag in one hand and brush in the other while he tried to quiet Blaze. The mare tossed her head saucily, stamped, and blew through her muzzle at him. Sara couldn't help laughing at the bewildered look on Sam's face.

"What's so funny?" he snapped.

"You are," giggled Sara. "You should see the expression on your face."

"I don't care how I look," grumbled Sam. "She won't stand still." He added with a sigh, "I don't know if I like this part of riding."

"It would help if you talk to Blaze while you groom her," Sara suggested, "then maybe she'll stand still."

She took the rub rag from Sam. Talking soothingly to the mare, while at the same time keeping a firm grip on the mane to keep the horse from tossing her head, Sara succeeded in getting Blaze quiet. Sam got to work with the brush and at last they were finished.

"How come you're so great with horses and I'm not?" Sam complained.

"Well, maybe it's because I understand them better," Sara replied, patting Blaze's neck.

"Or maybe it's because you think like a horse, Twinny," Sam teased, his good humor restored.

They shut the stall door, making sure it was bolted, and returned the equipment to the tack room. Bob wasn't anywhere around, but Sara knew that he would inspect their work later.

They got on their bikes that were parked outside the corral fence and pedaled up the road toward Marsh Pond Farm. They didn't talk much on the way home; they were both preoccupied with their own thoughts.

Sara was thinking about Dusty. Not only had she a horse to ride, but Bob had given her the responsibility of caring for Dusty. It was almost as if the mare were her own. Sara couldn't be happier.

Sam's thoughts were on a more sober subject. He kept thinking about what Huy had told them and wondered what they could do to help the two Vietnamese brothers.

"We have to tell Tim about Huy staying in the cabin," he said, "and warn him not to tell anyone."

"We'll tell him as soon as we get home," Sara said.

But it wasn't until later that night that the twins could get Tim alone long enough to talk to him. Huddled together on the bed in his room, they told him all about Huy and Dzung.

Tim brushed his fingers through his dark hair. "Wow, we got a real problem. I don't know how we can get the two brothers together, especially since Dzung's foster parents want only one foster son and not two."

"It's terrible to separate brothers," Sara reflected sadly. She looked at Sam and Tim. "Wouldn't it be awful if you two were separated?"

Sam glanced at Tim and a smile quirked one corner of his mouth. "Oh, I don't know," he teased.

Tim threw his pillow and Sam ducked.

"Come on, cut out the rough stuff," Sara admonished, "or Mom and Dad will be in here."

Tim retrieved his pillow, fluffed it, and slid it behind his back. "Okay, Superbrain," he asked Sam, "how can we help Huy and Dzung?"

Sam drew in a long breath. "I don't know," he said. "You guys have any ideas?"

Tim scrunched his forehead in concentration and gazed off into space while Sara sat on the edge of the bed, hugging her knees to her chin thoughtfully. Tim's noisy old alarm clock ticked loudly in the still night as they sat thinking.

It was so quiet in the room that a sudden loud noise outside startled them. Three heads turned to the open window as if jerked by a string.

"What was that?" Tim exclaimed.

"It sounded like a motorcycle roaring by," Sam replied, scrambling to the open window. Sara and Tim were by his side in an instant.

"This place is getting as bad as the city," Tim grumbled as they listened to the roar of the motor fade away in the distance. Sam made a wry face. "Well, at least you're in the front of the house and don't have to put up with frogs grumping away all night."

Sara looked out at the night. A half moon riding high in the sky brightened the yard and silvered the road beyond, like a satin ribbon wound around the dark hills. Silence again settled over the farm and she was about to turn from the window when the quiet of the night was shattered a second time by the sound of the motorcycle. The sound grew louder and louder as it came nearer.

"Hey, the guy's coming back," Tim said.

They kept their eyes on the road as they waited for the motorcycle to come into view. Then as the moonlight reflected on the silver cycle, Sam cried out, "It's Huy Chau's old motorcycle!"

"It sure looks like the one we found parked in the lean-to at the cabin," agreed Tim.

Sara tried to get a look at the rider, but the helmet with

73

the visor down covered his face. "Of course we can't be sure that was Huy," she said as the motorcycle roared out of sight again.

"It was Huy all right," Sam said with a firm nod.

"How can you be sure?" Sara protested. "You couldn't see the rider."

"How many other old silver-painted motorcycles like that one are around here?" Sam said, laughing. He sobered at once and shook his head, puzzled. "I wonder why Huy is riding up and down the road this time of night?"

Tim shrugged. "Maybe he does it for kicks."

Sam threw a glance at Tim's old alarm. "At eleven-thirty?"

Tim shook his head and turned away from the window. "I'm too bushed to do any more thinking tonight. How about you kids scramming so a guy can get some sleep."

The twins murmured their good nights and shut Tim's bedroom door quietly behind them. On their way down the hall to their own rooms, Sara said under her breath, "What do you really think Huy was doing, riding his motorcycle up and down the road this time of night?"

Sam twitched his shoulders. "Beats me. It wouldn't be my idea of kicks."

Sara wrinkled her brows. "When we go to Fox Ridge Farm tomorrow to exercise Dusty and Blaze, let's find out."

"Fine with me," Sam answered yawning. " 'Night, Twinny."

74

9

A Face in the Window

THE next afternoon Sara and Sam cycled down the road to Fox Ridge Farm. As before, they parked their bikes by the fence and walked across the corral. As they entered the stable, they could hear voices.

Bob Dolan and Mr. Raber were standing at Beauty's stall, talking in concerned tones. When the two men turned and saw them, Sara and Sam could tell by the troubled expressions on their faces that something was wrong.

The twins walked up to the stall. "How's Beauty?" Sam asked.

Mr. Raber shook his head dolefully, and Bob blurted out, "He's gone!"

Sara stared wide-eyed at the empty stall.

"We had another theft last night," Mr. Raber explained, his usual jovial face somber. "This morning Bob found Beauty's stall door open. Same as the last time when we found White Lightning missing."

For a moment the twins were too stunned by the news to say anything, then Sam asked, "Do you think it was the same horse thieves?"

Mr. Rader's eyes darkened. "Looks like it, and they were mighty sneaky, too. Bob slept in the tack room again last night, but he didn't hear a thing."

"We both turn in around ten," Bob told them, "so the thieves must have come after that."

"How did they get out of the corral with the gate locked?" Sam wondered.

. "The state police asked that same question this morning," Mr. Raber said, gesturing to the back door of the stable as he spoke. "They think the thieves led Beauty out the back way."

"They must have," Bob added, "or I would have heard them."

Mr. Raber frowned thoughtfully. "One thing is certain, they sure know how to handle horses to be able to get Beauty out of his stall without waking Bob here."

While Mr. Raber had been talking, Bob was working some loose straw on the floor into a little pile with the toe of his boot. Now he raised his sharp blue eyes and gave the twins a searching look. "You didn't hear anything out of the way or see anything suspicious go up the road past your place last night, did you?"

Sara wondered why Bob asked that question. Had he also heard Huy's motorcycle going up and down the road? She flashed her brother a quick look, but Sam's sober face remained wooden, his eyes guarded.

"After being used to city noises, all we notice here are the frogs," he answered evasively.

Sara let out a small sigh of relief. She was glad Sam didn't mention seeing Huy's motorcycle until they had a chance to talk to the Vietnamese boy.

Mr. Raber walked over to Black Cloud's stall and reached up to stroke the stallion's neck. The beautiful black horse nickered and shook his head. The muscles around Mr. Raber's mouth tightened. "I suppose they'll be after you next, Black Cloud."

"Not if I can help it," Bob spoke up. Then with a thin laugh, "I'll keep my eye on him even if I have to sleep in his stall."

Mr. Raber put a grateful hand on Bob's shoulder. After a minute he drew a long breath and said, "Well, there's nothing we can do now but get back to work."

"Would you like us to exercise Dusty and Blaze today?" Sara asked.

"I'd be glad if you would. That's Vicki's job when she's here. I sure do miss her." Mr. Raber managed to smile at the twins. "Bob tells me you're good riders, so ride anywhere you want to, so long as it's on Fox Ridge Farm property."

The heavy spirits caused by the discovery that Beauty was missing lifted a little as Sara went to the tack room for Dusty's bridle and saddle. Sam followed with Blaze's tack, and after the two horses were bridled and saddled, the twins rode out of the corral to find Huy.

At the upper end of the field, the Vietnamese youth dropped his fence stretcher and ran up to meet them. Before they could say a word, he asked eagerly, "Everything is okay? You talk to elder brother?"

"Everything's okay," Sam assured him. "Tim won't say anything. He wants to help, too."

Huy smiled with relief. "Is good. I thank you."

He was about to turn back to his work when Sara asked, "Do you know that Beauty is missing?"

Huy's smile quickly disappeared. He nodded gravely.

"By the way," Sam said, trying to make his voice sound casual, "we saw you riding your motorcycle up and down the road late last night. Did you see anything suspicious?"

Huy looked puzzled. "I not riding motorcycle last night."

"But it was your motorcycle we saw," Sam persisted.

Huy's face darkened and he shook his head. "You make mistake. I know nothing about this." His eyes slid away from theirs, and he turned to walk back to the fence.

Sara eyed him quizzically as she reined Dusty around. "Well, we better exercise these horses," she said. "See you around, Huy."

They jogged back across the field and walked their horses behind the barn, where Huy's motorcycle was parked.

Sam looked hard at the silver-painted cycle. "I'm sure this is the same cycle we saw last night."

Sara's attention was aroused by something else. "There's a worn track leading from the back of the barn here," she observed. "Let's follow it and find out where it takes us."

They rode up the narrow track away from the barn and discovered that it followed the top of the field along the outside of the fence.

"This must be the way Huy comes to the barn from the cabin," mused Sam. "He can't get through the fence at the end of the field so he has to use this path alongside it."

"Do you think the thieves used this track when they left the barn with Beauty?" asked Sara.

"I don't see why they would," Sam replied, "because this track is coming out at the woods road which just leads back to the cabin." In the next breath he said, "Let's ride back to the cabin, Sara. I'd like to look around some more when Huy's not around."

As they followed the old road through the tall ferns and low bushes, Sara asked, "Do you think Huy was telling the truth about not riding his motorcycle up and down the road last night?"

"How could he be telling the truth," Sam reasoned, "when it was his motorcycle we saw?"

"Then why didn't he admit it?" Sara persisted with a frown.

Sam shrugged. "I don't know, unless he had something to do with the robbery or saw something he didn't want to tell."

"But Huy wouldn't have anything to do with the robbery!" Sara's voice was almost a wail. She couldn't believe that Huy was in any way responsible for the missing Saddle-

"Someone's in the cabin!" Sara gasped. Sam frowned. "I don't see anyone," he said.

breds. Yet, she had to admit that she was puzzled that he had denied it was his motorcycle they had seen. She let out a long sigh. Maybe they would get some answers at the cabin.

When they reached the clearing, they wrapped the reins of their horses around two sturdy beech saplings on the edge of the woods. While Sam was making sure his bowline knot held, Sara started toward the cabin. Halfway across the clearing she stopped abruptly and stiffened.

"What's the matter?" Sam asked, running to catch up with her.

"Someone's in the cabin!" she gasped.

Sam frowned. "I don't see anyone."

"There!" Sara pointed a shaky finger. "There at the window! A face was looking out at us!"

10

Another Clue

SARA was tempted to run back to Dusty and ride away from the clearing as fast as she could go. Being a prisoner in the cellar hole had left a bad memory. She wasn't sure she wanted to go inside that cabin again, especially when a mysterious face had peered out at them through the window. But Sam grabbed her by the arm and hurried her the rest of the way across the clearing.

When they reached the cabin, they walked across the porch and Sam knocked on the door. When no one answered, he rapped again, much louder this time. While they waited for an answer, they listened for any movement inside the cabin, but there was none. A silence hung over the clearing as though the forest itself was holding its breath.

"Maybe you just imagined you saw a face in the window," Sam told Sara in a low whisper. "Maybe it was the reflection of a tree branch swaying in the breeze or a moving cloud."

"It was a face," insisted Sara. "A face with eyes, nose, and a mouth looking out the window at us. And when I pointed it out to you, it vanished."

Sam took an uneven breath. "Well, there's only one way to find out for sure and that's to go inside."

He pushed the door open with his foot and peered in at the one room of the cabin. The next moment he stepped inside and motioned for Sara to follow. The room was empty.

"There's no one here," Sam said, "so you must have seen an image reflected on the window and thought it was a face."

"Wait a minute," Sara told him. She walked over to the cot and getting down on her hands and knees, looked under it.

"Oh, Sara, come on!" laughed Sam.

Sara got up and brushed off her hands. "I'm sure there was someone in here," she insisted.

Her eyes flitted around the empty room. Suddenly her gaze fixed on the middle of the floor.

"There's only one other place to look."

With one accord they made for the trapdoor. Sam swung it back, and in the silence of the cabin it clattered loudly against the floor. Together they peered into the dark hole.

Sara put her finger to her lips. Was there a slight movement far back in a dark corner?

They exchanged puzzled glances. A second later Sam started down the ladder. "Be careful!" Sara whispered after him.

The cellar hole was cold and clammy, and Sara shivered

at the memory of having been trapped in there so recently. Her anxious eyes peered through the square opening to the dim room below and fixed on the old crocks and jars lined up along the wall just as they had been before. And there was the barrel that had stood in the corner. She looked hard at the barrel. She felt that something was wrong with it, and then she realized what it was. It had been moved away from the corner.

Taking a deep breath, she hissed, "Look behind the barrel, Sam."

No sooner had the words left her mouth than a figure leaped out of the darkness.

"Oh!" Sara gasped as the figure dodged past Sam and made for the ladder. "Who-who are you?" she stuttered with surprise as she stared down at the narrow, frightened face looking up at her.

Not giving the boy a chance to answer, Sam said crossly, "Get up that ladder!"

The boy obeyed and scrambled up the ladder with Sam close behind him. When they were out of the cellar hole, Sam turned the boy around so that they could get a better look at him.

He was about ten years old, they guessed, but small for his age. He had big brown eyes and blue-black hair that was covered with dust. He kept staring back at them with the same fearful and furtive expression that they had seen on Huy Chau's face the first time they had met him. At once they knew who he was.

"You're Dzung," Sara said. "Huy's brother."

The boy nodded, his lower lip trembling.

"We know Huy," Sara explained quickly. "We're his friends."

"Friends?" repeated the boy with surprise.

"Yeah, that's right," Sam said, grinning his crooked grin. "I'm Sam Harmon and this is my sister Sara. Sorry I yelled at you down in that cellar hole, but I almost flipped when you jumped out from behind that barrel."

"We'd like to help you and your brother," Sara explained.

"Help?" the boy questioned. Then he smiled. "Is good."

"Hey, you and Huy understand English pretty well," Sam said. "Where did you learn it?"

"Foster parents teach me. Huy learn from church sponsors. We know some English from refugee camps."

"Refugee camps?" asked Sara.

"Yes, refugee camps," came a voice from the doorway.

All three of them swung around in time to see Huy walking into the cabin. The older Vietnamese boy grinned at the surprised look on the twins' faces and explained, "I see you two riding through woods to cabin. I come quick so Dzung not be frightened."

"We didn't frighten him as much as he frightened us," declared Sara.

"Sara saw Dzung looking out the window at us and thought he was a ghost," laughed Sam.

"I did not think he was a ghost," Sara retorted, giving Sam a nudge with her elbow. Quickly changing the subject, she asked, "What about the refugee camps? Were you in many of them?"

"I'd like to hear how you two got out of Vietnam," Sam added. "That is, if you want to talk about it."

"I will tell you," Huy said. "Then you understand better why Dzung and I want to stay together." He settled himself cross-legged on the floor and the other three joined him.

"Dzung and I lived in Cholon, Chinese section of Saigon, now called Ho Chi Minh City. Our parents die; we live with old Grandmother. She save money to get us on small boat

84

from Saigon to Mekong Delta. Before we leave, old Grandmother make us promise always to stay together like brothers."

"And we promise," Dzung broke in, nodding solemnly at Sara and Sam.

Sara smiled at the sober little boy and moved closer to him as Huy went on to tell about his and Dzung's adventures.

He told about the fishing boat at the Mekong Delta that had taken them into the South China Sea and how they had to lie hidden on the bottom of the boat with the other refugees so that they could slip past the communist patrol boats, unnoticed. He told how they had sailed for Thailand on a Thai fishing boat and about the nightmare of being attacked by brutal pirates. After the pirates had taken all their food, water, and gasoline, they had left the passengers to die in the open sea. But with jerry-built sails made out of blankets and with four oars, they made their way toward shore.

After two days the boat crashed on rocks off the coast of Thailand, and some villagers cared for them until they could travel to a United Nations station, where they received clothing and "CARE" parcels. After being shuttled through five different refugee camps in Southeast Asia, Huy and Dzung finally got word that they had sponsors in the United States.

"Wow, what an adventure!" Sam exclaimed, his eyes shining with admiration for the Vietnamese brothers. "You two certainly were brave to stick through everything until you got here."

Huy bowed his head modestly. "Our troubles not over yet," he reminded them. "Then we had dangers, yes. But we were together like brothers. Now we are apart."

"We know," Sara said with a sigh.

Huy got up and looked fondly at his brother. "I go to work now, Dzung. Soon I be back."

Dzung smiled up at his big brother and nodded.

"We better go, too," Sara said. "We've been neglecting Dusty and Blaze."

They left the cabin and waved good-bye to the boy, standing small and solemn in the doorway. Sara mounted Dusty, and Sam gave Huy a hand up on Blaze. With another wave at Dzung, they rode out of the clearing.

After they left Huy at the field, they loped back to the stable and rubbed down Dusty and Blaze.

"I keep thinking about everything Huy told us," Sam said as he carefully bolted the door to Blaze's stall. "You know—about communist patrol boats and pirates and all. After all they've been through together, it's a rotten shame Huy and Dzung can't live like brothers as their grandmother wanted them to."

"I know," Sara said, an unhappy look in her hazel eyes. "I've been praying a lot for Huy and Dzung. That's the only help I can think of right now."

They got on their bikes by the corral fence and pedaled down the lane. When they reached the road, Sara asked, "Did you see any clues at the cabin that Huy was out with his motorcycle last night?"

Sam shook his head. "No, I didn't, but I'm sure that was Huy's motorcycle we saw, even though he denied it."

They pedaled along in silence for a while. They were coasting around the curve when Sara suddenly turned off the road and stopped.

"Let's cut across Green Meadow," she called back to Sam. "There's a track along the field we can follow. I wonder if it leads to the shed down by the woods."

Sam grinned. "I know! You want to show me that famous bridle you found there."

"Could be," Sara quipped.

She led the way along the far side of the field, the wheels of her bike bumping over the uneven ground. "This track must have been made by the machinery used to cut the hay," she explained over her shoulder. "Dad said Green Meadow is a hay field, and a farmer comes every summer to mow it."

"Well, the mowing machine certainly made enough ruts "

Sara's excited voice cut through Sam's complaints. "Look, there's the shed! Just as I thought."

They got off their bikes by the sliding door and kicked the kickstands down. Sam walked around the old building, observing it with a critical eye.

"This would make a neat studio for Mom," he agreed, "if it had a skylight. It could stand a coat of paint, too."

"Let's go inside. I'll show you that bridle," Sara said eagerly.

They pushed open the sliding door on its rusty rollers. As Sam gaped around at the interior of the shed, Sara led the way to the back. Underneath the loft she stopped short and blinked her eyes at the empty nail in the wall.

"It's gone!" she cried with surprise.

"What's gone?" Sam asked, absentmindedly examining the old hayrake. He looked up at Sara, then added quickly, "Oh, you mean the bridle you told me about."

Sara nodded, and a frown creased her forehead. "Someone must have taken it away."

"Most likely the person who left it there," Sam said logically. "He probably found out that we moved here and came for it."

87

"But why was it here in the first place," Sara wondered, "and why didn't he come to the house first and explain that he had left the bridle in the shed and ask if he could get it? I would have if I had left something in someone's shed." She pondered a moment, her lip caught between her teeth. "It looks as if whoever he was didn't want us to see him take the bridle away."

"You sure are making a big deal over it," Sam said, grinning at his sister. "And you got that gleam in your eye, Twinny. The gleam that tells me you are about to hatch a theory."

"I am," Sara announced. "I believe that the bridle I saw on this wall has something to do with Mr. Raber's missing stallions."

Sam blew air through his pursed lips. "Oh, wow! Isn't that a little far out, Sara? How do you figure?"

"Well," Sara said, warming up to her idea, "maybe this is where the horse thieves picked up the stolen Saddlebreds. After all, they couldn't just drive their horse van up to the stable at Fox Ridge Farm. Our shed can't be seen from the road. It would be the perfect place for the pickup."

Sam's brow wrinkled thoughtfully. "You might have something there, Sara," he muttered. "But how did they get White Lightning and Beauty here to this shed?"

"Someone rode them here from Fox Ridge Farm," Sara said simply. "Don't you see? The bridle I found hanging on the wall proves they had been ridden here. Then last night when Beauty was brought here, the thief discovered he had left the bridle behind and remembered to take it with him this time."

She paused, her eyes appraising the space underneath the loft. "The stallions could have been kept under the loft until the van came for them. There's plenty of space for that."

Sam stood for a moment, turning Sara's ideas over in his mind. Then his eyes lighted up. "You know, you have a good theory there, Sara. Now all we have to do is find out who it was who rode the horses from the Fox Ridge stable to this shed."

"And how he got here," Sara added. "He certainly didn't ride the Saddlebreds up the road in full view of Fox Ridge Farm."

Sam nodded agreement. "But if he didn't take the road," he wondered, "how did he get the Saddlebreds from Fox Ridge Farm to this shed?"

Perplexed, they looked at one another for a long moment. Then Sam turned to look around the shed some more.

Sara was about to follow him when a bit of color on the floor boards underneath the loft caught her eye. Reaching down, she picked up a large handkerchief patterned with red and black squares. It was such a gaudy thing that she wondered how she could have missed seeing it before. But then, she hadn't been looking at the floor. Her eyes had focused on the empty nail on the wall that had held the bridle.

"Look at this," she said as she showed Sam the gaudy handkerchief. "I found it on the floor just now. Look how big it is. It must be a man's handkerchief."

When Sam saw the handkerchief, his voice rose with excitement. "Hey, it looks familiar! I'm sure I've seen a handkerchief like this one before, and it wasn't long ago." He kept staring at the red-and-black-checkered handkerchief. "I know I saw it *somewhere*."

"Well, try to remember," Sara urged, getting more excited as she talked. "It may be an important clue."

"I know—I know." Sam struck his hand against his forehead and groaned in an agonized voice, "Where in the world did I see this handkerchief? Why can't I remember?"

89

11

Sam Remembers

WHEN they reached home, Sam put the handkerchief Sara had found in his chest of drawers under a pile of T-shirts. "Another clue," he told Sara, then he continued in a frustrated voice, "If I could only remember where I saw it before!"

During dinner that night they talked about Beauty's disappearance. "That's the second stallion that's missing from Fox Ridge Farm," Sara informed her parents and Tim.

Mrs. Harmon shook her head. "I wonder what has happened to those two horses?"

"Mr. Raber thinks a gang of horse thieves took them because other stables near here have also reported missing thoroughbreds," replied Sam.

Tim had been listening quietly to the conversation. Suddenly he came alert. "Hey, we heard Huy's motorcycle going up and down the road late last night. I wonder if he saw anything connected with the robbery."

Sam shook his head. "Sara and I asked him, and he said he didn't know anything. In fact he told us he wasn't riding his motorcycle last night."

Tim sat forward, his black eyebrows drawn into a frowning line. "I can't figure it. That was his motorcycle we saw."

Mrs. Harmon spoke up just then. "Now who is this Huy? I know you mentioned him before but I've forgotten what you said about him."

"He's a Vietnamese refugee who works for Mr. Raber," Tim replied.

Sara held her breath, hoping that Tim wouldn't make a slip and tell Mom and Dad about Huy running away from his sponsors in Philadelphia and hiding in the cabin across the pond. Just in time Tim caught the look Sara flashed across the table at him and stopped talking abruptly.

There was a long pause, then Dad said, shaking his head, "That's too bad for Ed Raber. I hope he soon locates his missing Saddlebreds."

Mrs. Harmon added in a voice full of concern, "I wish we could do something for him."

Suddenly Sara sat up, her eyes shining. "Maybe we can, Mom. Let's have a cookout tomorrow night and invite Mr. Raber and Bob Dolan. That might cheer them up."

Her mother turned to her, smiling. "Why that's a wonderful idea, honey."

Dad chuckled. "I guess Ed and Bob will be glad to get away from their own cooking for one night. I know I would."

"Then it's settled," Mrs. Harmon said. "I'll call Ed right

91

after dinner." Turning to her husband, she asked, "Now, dear, how did your meeting at the college go today?"

"Fine," their father replied. "I met several men in the history department. Jim Burton has invited us to attend his church tomorrow."

Tim leaned back in his chair with a frown. "Do we have to go to church so soon, Dad?"

Professor Harmon flashed a surprised look at his son. "You know we attend church every Sunday, Tim."

"I know we did back in Philly, but we're new here and don't know anyone yet."

"Church is the best place to meet new friends," his mother told him.

Sara suppressed a giggle. "And with all that charm of yours, Tim, you shouldn't have trouble making friends."

"Especially girls," Sam teased.

"Oh, buzz off, you two," Tim grumbled, but he didn't say any more about not wanting to go to church.

The next morning as they rode through Maplewood, Sara looked out the windows of the station wagon at the pretty little town. It was aptly named, she thought, as she gazed at the tall maple trees that lined the main street. At the square, Professor Harmon turned on the street that curved up the hill to the college buildings.

"We're a little early for church, so let's take a quick look at the campus," he said.

He stopped in front of a gray stone building half-covered with ivy. "That's the history building," he told them. "My office is on the first floor, right inside the door."

"What a pretty campus," Mrs. Harmon remarked. "I would just love to paint your building sometime, John."

Professor Harmon drove through the campus, then back to the town square. He parked the station wagon a block away from the square and led the way to a red brick church with a tall white spire.

As soon as the Harmons settled themselves into a pew and sang the familiar opening hymn, they began to feel at home. Worshiping God was the same everywhere, Sara thought, as she listened to the familiar Bible verses the minister read.

Pastor Reese was a small man with a fringe of gray hair and a gentle face. But there was a lively sparkle in his blue eyes when he shook Sara's hand at the door after the service.

"We're so glad to meet new worshipers and hope we'll see you young people next Sunday," he told her.

"Oh, we'll be here," Sara promised. She liked the friendly little minister and his welcoming smile.

A square-shouldered, stocky young man with a pleasant face hurried over to meet them. "I'm glad you could come today," he said. "I'd like you to meet my family."

Jim Burton introduced his pretty young wife, his two small daughters, Jennifer and Lisa, and Dzung, whose dark eyes brightened when he saw Sara and Sam.

"Dzung is our foster son," Professor Burton said as he slipped his arm around the boy's shoulders. "He joined our family several months ago."

Dzung looked up at his foster father with a big smile. Sara could see that there was a lot of love between them.

"The girls are delighted to have a big brother," Mrs. Burton added.

At the mention of "big brother," the little girls tugged at Dzung's hands to draw him away from the grown-ups to the swings in the grassy area behind the Sunday school. Sara smiled as she watched them go. She was happy that Dzung had a loving foster family. Now if only Huy could somehow be close to his brother, she knew that Dzung's happiness would be complete.

They said good-bye to the Burtons, and after Professor Harmon called to Tim, who was talking to two giggling girls his own age, they got into the station wagon and started for home.

"You know, I think I'm going to like Maplewood," Tim said with a smug smile on the way back to the farm.

* * *

After Sunday dinner, Sam and Tim helped their father get out the grill and charcoal for the cookout. Then, laden with tubes of caulking, paintbrushes, and cans of paint, the boys went down to the dock to spruce up the old rowboat. After Sara helped her mother with the salad and dessert, she joined them.

"How do you like her, Sara?" Tim asked. *"She's all caulked and painted and ready to be launched as soon as she dries."*

When Tim saw her coming through the woods, he pointed to the rowboat and said with unabashed pride, "How do you like her, Sara? She's all caulked and painted and ready to be launched as soon as she dries."

The boys had managed to get the boat onto the dock, and now it looked bright and shining with its coat of blue paint and white trim. The bright colors reminded Sara of the saucy kingfishers that flew around the pond, and she exaulted, "She's as pretty as a kingfisher! That's what we'll call her—*The Kingfisher*."

"Oh, no!" Tim groaned. "Do we have to give her a name, too?"

"Of course," Sara said. "All boats have names."

Sam said with a grin, "I'll letter the name on her bow, Sara, as soon as the paint's dry."

Sara admired the rowboat some more, then told her brothers they had better get ready for the cookout. Tim cleaned the brushes with turpentine and put the lids on the two cans of paint.

"I'm hungry enough to eat a dozen of Dad's grilled steaks," he said.

"So am I," Sam agreed as he picked up the empty caulking tubes and the putty knives.

"You better leave some for the guests," laughed Sara as they started up through Hemlock Woods.

While the boys showered and put on clean clothes, Sara sat on the side porch to keep an eye open for their guests. At exactly five-thirty the red van drove into the driveway and parked in front of the barn.

"Here they are!" she announced.

At her call the boys thundered down the back stairs, and Professor and Mrs. Harmon came out on the side porch to greet their guests.

Mr. Raber looked dapper in his western hat and his tan sport jacket. Bob Dolan had on a long-sleeved cowboy shirt and wore a pair of shiny new western boots. His blond curly hair was brushed neatly, and he looked younger, somehow, and quite handsome.

Mr. Raber beamed at them all. "Well, this is mighty nice of you folks to have us over for supper. Sure beats eating canned beans, doesn't it, Bob?"

Bob Dolan nodded. "Sure does."

Professor Harmon put the steaks on the grill, and Mr. Raber helped turn them.

"I always grill the steaks at home," he told Mrs. Harmon as she began to protest that he was the guest and shouldn't be working. "I like doing it."

"He has a feel for when a steak is just right," Bob praised. "You know, when it's just rare enough to sink your teeth into."

Mr. Raber laughed heartily and when the steaks were done, he took out his handkerchief to wipe the perspiration off his red face. As he helped Dad lift the steaks onto a large oval platter, he accidentally dropped the handkerchief on the grass.

Sam's eye was quick to notice it. He jumped as if he were stung by a bee. Sara let out a screech as he almost knocked over the bowl of salad.

When he retrieved the handkerchief, she hissed under her breath, "What was all that about, Sam? You almost dumped the salad all over me."

"I'll tell you later," he mumbled between closed lips.

The rest of the evening went smoothly. After they ate, they sat around the glowing grill and talked until it got dark and the mosquitoes started buzzing around their heads. When Mrs. Harmon suggested that they go inside, Mr.

96

Raber thanked her but said, "Bob and I have some work to do in the stable before we turn in, and I don't like to be away too long because of those horse thieves."

"I can understand that," Professor Harmon said. "We hope they are soon caught and your Saddlebreds are back again in their own stable."

Mr. Raber nodded soberly, then he and Bob thanked their hosts for the cookout and drove off in the red van.

After the twins had helped their parents clean up, Sam motioned for Sara to follow him up the back stairway. Shutting the door to his room behind them, he went to his chest and pulled out the bottom drawer.

While he rummaged under his T-shirts, Sara asked, "You sure have been acting queer all evening, Sam. What do you want to show me?"

Sam pulled out the large red-and-black-checkered handkerchief she had found in the shed. "It's this," he said, holding out the gaudy handkerchief. "I remember now where I had seen it before."

"Where?" asked Sara breathlessly.

"In Mr. Raber's jacket pocket, the day Tim and I followed the woods road to Fox Ridge Farm. You weren't with us then. Remember? You were in the cellar hole."

"How can I forget!" Sara shuddered.

"Well, anyway," Sam went on, "Mr. Raber was bringing Black Cloud to Fox Ridge Farm. He was dressed up that day, too, and wore the same tan sport jacket he wore tonight. But instead of a plain, white handkerchief tucked in the breast pocket, he had this one."

"So that's why you almost dumped the salad in my lap when Mr. Raber dropped his handkerchief!" Sara exclaimed.

"Yeah, it all came back to me then," Sam told her. "But

what I can't understand is what was Mr. Raber's handkerchief doing in the shed where you found the bridle?"

Sara blinked her eyes thoughtfully. "Maybe the bridle
didn't belong to the horse thieves after all. Maybe it was Mr.
Raber's and when he came for it, he dropped the handkerchief." She bit her lips and frowned. "But then that lets
out our theory that the shed was used as a meeting place for
the thieves who stole the Saddlebreds."

"I know," Sam said, tossing the handkerchief back into
his drawer.

Sara sank down on Sam's lumpy bed. Her expression was
one of dismay. "That means we're right back where we
started from. We scored a big zilch!"

"Not exactly, Sara. We now know who the handkerchief
belongs to."

"A lot of good that is," grumbled Sara. "Mr. Raber
wouldn't steal his own Saddlebreds."

The twins looked despairingly at one another. "I guess
you're right," Sam said with a heavy sigh. "Back to square
one."

12

The Marked Trail

TIM tested the paint once more to make sure *The King-fisher* was completely dry before they edged the rowboat off the dock and into the water.

"We forgot to paint the oars," Sam said ruefully as he slipped them into the oarlocks.

"No sweat," replied Tim. "We can paint them in the barn after dinner."

It was a beautiful afternoon, several days later. A good day to launch *The Kingfisher*, they decided. Tim, assuming the air of captain, seated himself in the middle of the boat where he could man the oars while Sara perched on the little seat in the bow and Sam leaped into the stern after pushing them off.

"You're the navigator," Tim called over his shoulder to Sara. "Keep a sharp lookout for stumps sticking out of the water. We wouldn't want to chip any paint off the bow of this fine ship."

"Aye, aye, captain," Sara replied with a mock salute. Turning in her seat, she directed Tim past several old tree stumps by shouting, "A little to the starboard, now a little to port."

"Wow, we got a real 'old tar' aboard," laughed Sam.

When they reached the middle of the pond, Tim asked, "Where to, mates?"

"Let's row over to the cabin," Sara suggested.

"What for?" asked Sam. "Huy won't be there. It's not his day off."

"Well, maybe Dzung will be there," Sara said. "He probably gets lonely, waiting for Huy to finish work. We could take him for a cruise around the pond."

"To the cabin it is," proposed Tim, looking around the bushy shoreline for a good place to beach the boat.

"There's a spot over there where there aren't so many reeds," Sara said, directing Tim toward an opening along the shore. She grabbed a hemlock bough to pull them in to the grassy bank.

After *The Kingfisher* touched shore, Sara leaped out, and Tim threw her the painter. She held the rope taut while the boys climbed out of the boat; then Tim looped the painter around the trunk of a hemlock so that *The Kingfisher* wouldn't drift away.

Sam led the way through a thick grove of rhododendron that ended in a patch of pines below the clearing. When they reached the cabin, they called Dzung's name several times. Hearing no response, Sara stepped up on the sagging porch and pushed open the door.

100

"Dzung, it's us," she called. "Sara and Sam." But there was still no answer.

Sara hesitated on the doorstep. "You don't think he's hiding in the cellar hole again?"

Sam shook his head. "He knows us now. If he were here, he'd answer."

They glanced around the cabin briefly, then headed back to The Kingfisher.

"My turn to row," Sam declared, stepping into the boat and claiming the middle seat.

Sara got into the stern this time and held tightly to the sides of the boat as Tim gave it a mighty shove and jumped into the bow.

"Let's row around the inlet," Sam suggested, awkwardly splashing the oars in the water and whacking a mossy stump in the process. "We haven't explored that side of the pond yet."

"If we get there without drowning," Tim muttered, grimacing at Sam's clumsy attempts at rowing.

Suddenly Sara let out a cry.

"Now what?" asked Tim, sitting up with a start.

"Look at that blue heron!" Sara breathed, pointing to a big blue bird with long skinny legs standing in the water.

Tim relaxed. "Oh, only a bird. I thought you had seen a sea monster. Forgot you were a bird-lover, Sara."

Sam let the oars trail in the water while they watched the heron unfold its long wings and sail off to the top of a hemlock. Tim squinted as he looked up at the bird. "How can it perch on the very top of a tree like that? You'd hardly know it was there unless you saw it fly up."

"One of God's wonders," Sara explained. "It's able to camouflage itself on that treetop for protection."

They watched the heron for a while, then Sam made a

zigzag path across the pond past the inlet. Tim, alert in the bow, warned, "Hey, you're heading straight for shore, Sam!"

Sam grunted as he tried to maneuver around a half-submerged stump. Sara came to her twin's rescue by suggesting, "Let's explore that cove on our side of the pond. A little more to the starboard, Sam."

Sam aimed the bow toward the dark inlet, narrowly avoiding another stump.

When at last they drifted into the green shade of the cove, Sara looked up through the tall trees and sighed with delight. "What a scene this would be for Mom to paint! And look at that pretty spring coming down through the woods."

"Let's get out and explore," said Tim. "My nerves need a rest after Sam's wild rowing."

They tied *The Kingfisher* to a hemlock bough and scrambled up over the roots of the tree onto the shore. The spring made a shallow depression through the woods, and they followed it until it disappeared under the roots of a giant beech tree.

"The water comes out of the ground here, then flows down to the pond," Sam informed them, getting down on his hands and knees and peering under the roots of the big tree. "Actually, that's how the pond is fed, with springs like this one all along its banks."

While the boys were examining the outlet of the spring, Sara walked around the beech and studied the woods around her. It was then that she spied a thin trail winding through the trees. "Hey, I found a trail," she called to her brothers. "Let's follow it and find out where it goes."

"Looks like a deer run to me," Tim observed when the boys joined her. "It'll probably lead us all over the place but let's go."

They started up the trail. Sam, who had been lagging along behind them, suddenly called out, "This is no deer run. It's a marked trail."

Sara and Tim stopped with surprise and stared back at him. "What do you mean?" Tim asked.

"You two have been looking down at the trail all the time and not up at the trees around you," Sam chided, pointing to a white mark painted on the trunk of a maple. "There's another one, Tim, right by your shoulder."

Tim swung around and stared at the long white blaze painted on the tree next to him. Several yards ahead they could see another white mark standing out boldly in the dimness of the woods.

"Now why would anyone want to mark this trail?" Sara puzzled. "It's easy enough to follow without marking it."

"It wouldn't be at night," Sam said thoughtfully. "If this trail is what I think it is, it'll lead up to the shed in the corner of the hayfield."

"Well, let's find out," Tim said, turning and assuming the lead as they followed the white blaze marks on the trees. A short time later he stopped in the middle of the trail and pointed ahead. "You're right, Sam. There's the shed. You can see it through the trees."

Sara stared at the familiar old shed and the hayfield beyond. Then she looked back at the marked trail and caught her breath. She was beginning to understand now what Sam had meant by the white blaze marks making the trail easy to follow at night.

"We may have been right after all, Sam." Her voice held a tense excitement. "Maybe the shed was used by the horse thieves. And this trail was how they brought White Lightning and Beauty from Fox Ridge Farm to the shed."

"That's what I was thinking," Sam exclaimed.

Tim looked at the twins somewhat blankly. "What are you two talking about?"

Quickly they informed Tim about their theory of how the old shed was used as a pickup place for the missing stallions.

"Finding Mr. Raber's handkerchief there the other day threw us off," Sara told him, "but this trail proves that somebody's been coming to the shed and probably at night."

Tim ran his fingers through his dark hair and gave them a searching look. "You know, you might have something there, and finding that handkerchief makes Mr. Raber, himself, a suspect."

Sara's eyes widened. "But why would Mr. Raber steal his own horses?"

Tim's brow furrowed as he glanced up at the old shed. "Well, he could be in with the horse thieves and had his own horses stolen to make himself look like a victim, so that nobody would suspect him."

Sara gave a hoot. "Oh, Tim, you've been reading too many who-done-its." She turned to Sam. "You saw how upset Mr. Raber was when he found Beauty missing."

Sam nodded thoughtfully, quietly digesting this new angle of Tim's. "I can't see Mr. Raber stealing his own Saddlebreds, but you have to admit that it does look like an inside job."

"What do you mean by that?" asked Sara.

"I mean whoever rode those stallions over this trail at night had to know all about Fox Ridge Farm and these woods and our shed."

Tim raised his eyebrows. "Right! And you have to admit that makes Mr. Raber a suspect."

Sara shrugged off Tim's suspicion. She still couldn't imagine Mr. Raber stealing his own Saddlebreds. She frowned down at the trail, and at that moment her eyes focused on something that made her exclaim, "Look at this!"

The three bent over to scrutinize the print of a horseshoe on a bare patch of ground. "And there's another one," Sara said, pointing. "They look as if they were made recently."

Tim's eyes narrowed as he studied the prints. "You know," he said, "I just had a thought. Could we be building this thing up? I mean, maybe this is just one of the Fox Ridge Farm riding trails."

Sara shook her head emphatically. "No, it isn't. All the Fox Ridge Farm trails are on Mr. Raber's land."

"Okay," Tim said with a shrug. "It was just an idea. The only thing I know to do now is to backtrack and find out where the trail takes us."

They turned and followed the marked trail back to the spring. From there it swung inland on higher ground as it circled the swampy inlet. As they had suspected, it came out at the woods road which led to Fox Ridge Farm.

"A roundabout way to get to the shed in our hayfield," mused Sam as they sat on a fallen log to rest, "but a safe way, if you don't want to be seen from the road."

"Remember Mr. Raber saying that the state police thought Beauty was let out the back door of the stable," Sara reminded her twin.

Sam nodded.

"Well," Sara went on, "the thief probably rode the stolen stallions along that track we found behind the barn the other day. You know, Sam, the track that follows the upper fence by the field and comes out at the woods road."

Sam nodded his head and added, "Then from the woods road the thief turned onto the trail here which leads to our shed. A perfect way to get the stolen Saddlebreds to the shed without being seen."

Sara got to her feet abruptly. "Oh wow! We almost got the mystery solved. I can't wait until we tell Mr. Raber."

"Not yet, Sara," Sam warned. "We don't tell anyone yet, not even Mom and Dad."

Tim nodded in agreement. "I'll go along with that. If it's an inside job, we wouldn't want to tip off the wrong person."

"Still thinking about Mr. Raber," Sara said as they started back to the cove where they had left *The Kingfisher.*

Tim twitched his shoulders. "At this point, Sara, it could be anyone."

"Tim's right," Sam agreed. "We got to have proof before we say anything."

When they arrived at the cove, Sara stepped into *The Kingfisher* first and claimed the middle seat. "It's my turn to row," she announced.

Tim looked skeptical as he pushed them off and leaped into the bow. But his worried frown disappeared as he watched Sara dip the oars into the water and row out of the cove with smooth, easy strokes.

"Hey, you row all right for a girl," he exclaimed with surprise.

Sara bristled at Tim's chauvinistic remark. "Why shouldn't a girl row just as well as a boy?" she flung back. "After all, I didn't go to camp all those years just to sit by the lake and enjoy the scenery."

"Okay, okay. Sorry if I offended," Tim said in a laughing voice.

While they were bantering back and forth, Sam sat in thoughtful silence. After a while Sara looked up from her rowing and noticed that faraway look on his face. Suddenly their eyes met, and one corner of Sam's mouth lifted into a grin.

"Come on, Sam," she said, grinning back at him, "I know that look. You just got a neat idea, haven't you?"

Sam nodded but remained mute.

Tim spoke up, "I'll bet you figured out who rode White Lightning and Beauty up that trail at night."

"I have an idea," replied Sam with a secretive look.

"Well, who was it?" Sara asked.

Sam remained agonizingly silent.

"Come on, Sam, tell us," she begged.

When Sam only shook his head and grinned at her, Sara lost her patience and splashed the water with her oar.

"Hey, you're getting me all wet," he yelled.

Sara held her dripping oar in the air threateningly. "I'll get you wetter, Sam, if you don't tell us."

"I actually don't know for sure," Sam said, ducking his head quickly to avoid the spray of water from Sara's oar. "I don't have all the pieces to the puzzle yet. All I can tell you is that I think Huy's motorcycle is a very important clue."

"In what way? Tim asked. "You don't think Huy's the thief!"

"I mean I think his motorcycle was used as a decoy," Sam explained.

"A decoy!" Sara and Tim trilled.

"Right. You know, to throw everyone off the real crook."

"But-but," Sara sputtered.

"I'm not saying any more," Sam said firmly, "because if my powers of deduction are wrong, it may get an innocent person into trouble. All I can say is if we hear that motorcycle going up and down the road again at night, we better get to that old shed and keep our eyes open."

"Then will we find the answer?" asked Sara.

"I hope so," Sam answered, grinning mysteriously at both of them.

13

The Thieves Strike Again

A FTER dinner Sara helped her mother clear the table and do the dishes while the boys went to the barn to paint the oars. Their father went with them.

"I'd like to start cleaning out this barn," Dad said, looking around at the junk stored in the dark corners. "We have to find room for that used tractor Mr. Raber is selling us. I want to have everything ready for when we start plowing your mother's garden."

"Isn't it a little late in the year to be thinking about a garden?" Tim asked.

"It may be too late to plant," their father answered, "but it's a good time to get part of the field cleared and the ground ready for next year's planting."

"Mom must be planning quite a garden, Dad," said Sam. Professor Harmon nodded. "Your mother and I want to grow as much of our own food as we can, and you boys and Sara can help. One of the reasons for buying this small farm is to cut down on food costs. Anyway, it'll be good for all of us to work the soil together."

"When do we start on Project Barn?" asked Tim.

"First thing tomorrow morning," their father told them. "With a good cleaning out and some minor repairs, this old barn won't look half bad."

"Oh, wow," moaned Sam. "That's going to be a lot of work."

" 'Whatever your hand finds to do, do it with all your might,' " Professor Harmon quoted from the Bible. He smiled at his sons and added, "Work will keep you from getting bored and missing your busy social lives in Philadelphia."

For the rest of the week they cleaned, hammered, and sawed. Sara and Mrs. Harmon helped with the project. By the end of the second week the old stone barn had been cleaned out, repaired, and its woodwork shone with a fresh coat of white paint.

"You see what good results can be had when everyone pitches in to help," Professor Harmon said with satisfaction the night they had finished the barn. They all agreed, even Sam whose thumbnail had turned black where he had hammered it by mistake.

"I'm turning in early," Tim said with a yawn. "I'm bushed."

"I won't be far behind," Sam told his brother as he closed the book he was falling asleep over.

Like her brothers, Sara was so tired that night that she didn't bother to hang up her clothes. She just tossed her jeans and shirt over a chair and climbed into bed. As soon as her head touched the pillow, she was sound asleep.

It seemed only a short time later that something woke her. She sat up and blinked her eyes sleepily. There it was again—a loud noise outside her open window.

Sara leaped out of bed and hurried to the window seat. The noise sounded fainter now as it faded away in the distance. Was it a truck that had passed by? she wondered. But it didn't have the deep rumble of a truck. It sounded more like—a motorcycle!

Sara ran out of her room and across the hall. She knocked softly, but urgently, on Sam's door. When he didn't answer, she opened the door and slipped into the room.

"Sam!" she hissed, giving his shoulder a shake. "Sam! Wake up!"

With a groan her twin rolled over. "W-what's the matter?" he mumbled sleepily.

"I think I heard a motorcycle go up the road just now."

At her words Sam's eyes popped wide open. He threw his covers aside and followed Sara to her room. Sara shut her door softly so that they wouldn't awaken their parents, then led the way to her window. They squatted on the window seat and peered out into the dark night.

"Did you get a look at it?" asked Sam. "Was it Huy's motorcycle?"

"I don't know," Sara replied. "The sound woke me up, and by the time I got to the window it had gone by."

"Well, if it was like last time, it'll come back," Sam reasoned.

They crouched together on the window seat and waited. Sara wasn't a bit sleepy now, and she knew that Sam wasn't either. Excitement coursed through their veins, keeping them wide awake and alert.

110

Suddenly Sam strained forward, cocking his ear expectantly. Then Sara heard it too—the distant, whining sound of a motor that grew louder and louder. They kept their eyes on the road, and when the motorcycle roared by again, they could just make out the helmeted figure riding it. In the glow of the headlight, they glimpsed the silver fender and wheel.

"It's Huy's all right," Sam whispered. "Come on, let's get to the shed. And hurry!"

"You mean it's the horse thieves again?" gasped Sara.

Sam gave her a quick bob of his head and raced back to his room to dress. Sara scrambled into her shirt and jeans and wiggled her feet into her old sneakers. Grabbing a sweater, she ran into the hall at the same time that Sam came hurrying out of his room. Quietly they closed their doors behind them and started down the back stairs.

"What about Tim?" Sara asked in a hushed voice, pausing on the top step and glancing back at their brother's room.

"You know it's next to impossible to awaken Tim when he's sound asleep," Sam whispered urgently. "We may be too late now as it is."

Sara nodded hesitantly and followed Sam down the stairs. They made their way across the kitchen to the back door. Sam unlocked the night latch, and as they slipped across the porch, Sara still felt guilty that they hadn't tried to awaken Tim. After all, she thought, he was in on this, too. But as she sped through the dark night after Sam, she realized that he was right. They hadn't a minute to lose.

There was only the starlight to guide them across the field, but soon their eyes became accustomed to the darkness and it wasn't long before they made out the faint outline of the shed. Suddenly Sam grabbed Sara's arm and pulled her

111

*In the glare of the high-powered flashlight the rider was holding
in front of him, they could make out the horse.*

into a clump of trees alongside the field. They had no sooner
reached the shelter of a drooping hemlock than Sam pointed
to a light wavering through the woods behind the shed.

They kept their eyes fixed on the light. As it came closer,
they heard the soft thud of a horse's hoofs on the marked
trail leading to the shed. Sara drew in her breath sharply. In
the glare of the high-powered flashlight the rider was holding in front of him, they could make out the horse. It was the
big stallion, Black Cloud!

They pressed back into the shadows of the hemlock as the
rider passed by and rode the stallion to the front of the shed.
He dismounted and knocked three times on the sliding door.
Immediately it slid open and the horse and rider disappeared inside.

Sara felt numb all over as she crouched under the hemlock close to Sam. Her twin said in a guarded voice, "Now

we know for sure that the thieves are using our shed as a pickup."

"But who was the rider?" Sara asked in a hushed, frightened voice. "It was too dark to get a good look at him."

"Let's sneak up to the shed and find out," Sam ventured. "There's that wide crack in the sliding door that we can look through."

They were about to leave their hiding place in the woods when a quick movement in the shadows of the trail brought them up short.

"Look!" breathed Sara as the movement took form and a dark figure tore itself from the woods and moved swiftly to the front of the shed. The next moment they heard the rasping squeak of the sliding door and a familiar voice call out: "My motorcycle—where is?"

A hand reached out and pulled the angry boy into the shed. A moment later the sliding door squeaked shut.

"They got Huy!" gasped Sam.

Quickly the twins slipped out from under the dark trees and made their way to the shed. They crept up to the wide crack in the door and peered into the dimly lit interior. They saw Huy standing before a slim young man with shaggy brown hair and wearing a beat-up denim jacket. The man was nervously turning the motorcycle helmet around in his hands.

"Why you take motorcycle?" Huy was accusing. "Who are you?"

The man didn't answer but glanced at the back of the shed where Black Cloud gave an indignant whinny. A dark form emerged from underneath the loft, and when it moved into the beam of the flashlight, Sara caught her breath with a hiss.

She stood rooted to the spot, her mind refusing to believe

113

what she saw. "Bob Dolan!" Her voice was a shaky whisper. They stared, unblinking, as Huy took several faltering steps backward, away from the man holding Black Cloud's bridle.

"Well, Huy," Bob Dolan said, his usual friendly face molded into a hard smile, "what are you doing here this time of night?"

"My motorcycle," Huy replied, pointing to the battered old cycle propped against the wall of the shed. "Why you steal?"

"I didn't steal your motorcycle," Bob said sarcastically. "I just borrowed it for Bert here to ride up and down the road." He turned with a harsh laugh to the other man. "You like riding beaten-up cycles at night, don't you, Bert?"

Bert grinned and nodded.

Huy looked bewildered. "I no understand."

Bob took a step toward Huy and said in a mocking voice, "Well, you see it's like this, kid. You and Bert are about the same size and with that helmet visor to hide Bert's face, nobody would know it was him and not you riding up and down the road the nights the stallions disappear."

Huy stared at Bob and then at the black stallion that moved restlessly underneath the loft.

"You-you steal Black Cloud!" he accused, his voice shrill and trembling.

Bob's face hardened. "So what? When I tell Mr. Raber about hearing your motorcycle tonight, he'll start to wonder. Maybe by now the Harmons have heard it and will begin to wonder, too."

"Mr. Raber not believe you!" cried Huy.

Bob laughed a nasty laugh. "It's my word against yours, Huy, and Mr. Raber's not likely to believe a runaway gook who's been hiding in his cabin. But he'll believe me all right."

114

He swung the bridle around in his hand and turned to Bert. "I won't forget the bridle this time. Now I got to be getting back to the stable. I'm supposed to be sound asleep in the tack room."

"What do I do with this kid?" Bert asked, pointing a thumb toward Huy.

Bob's sharp blue eyes studied the Vietnamese boy for a moment, then he said, "Maybe it'll be better if he disappears suddenly. Then he'll look more guilty than ever. Take him with you when Charlie comes with the van. The boss will know what to do with him."

With that Bob turned and was about to start for the sliding door when Huy sprang forward blocking his way. "You no steal Black Cloud!" His breath came in short, angry gasps. "I not let you!"

Bob's fist flew into Huy's stomach, knocking the wind out of the boy and sending him reeling backward from the blow.

"Now get out of my way, Huy," snapped Bob, "or next time you won't know what hit you."

Beside her Sara could feel Sam stiffen. "We got to help Huy," he rasped.

She knew that Sam wanted to push open the shed door that very moment and go to Huy's rescue. She reached out to grab his arm.

"Wait!" she whispered shrilly. "We won't be any help to Huy if they get us, too. It would only make matters worse for all of us."

No sooner had she spoken when, through the crack, they glimpsed Bob walking toward the door. Just in time Sara pulled Sam out of sight around the corner of the shed. They pressed their backs against the rough wooden boards and held their breath as Bob's light wavered past them. They stood perfectly still until the sound of his footsteps disap-

115

peared down the trail that led to the old woods road.

Then in a rush of words Sam said, "I'm going in there, Sara. Together Huy and I ought to be able to handle Bert."

His voice was determined, and Sara knew that there was no stopping him this time. He started for the front of the shed, but just as quickly drew back into the shadows again as the hayfield sprang into light.

Two bright beams bobbed along the track at the edge of the field as a horse van came into view. The driver negotiated a half turn in the field and backed up to the shed door. The headlights flickered off, but the engine kept purring.

Immediately the sliding door was opened, and Bert was hurrying Huy to the cab of the van. By the awkward way Huy moved, Sara was sure that his hands were tied behind his back and a blindfold covered his eyes.

After a few words with Bert, the driver pulled Huy into the cab and stayed with him while Bert went back to the shed for Black Cloud.

It was while Bert was in the shed that a sudden idea popped into Sara's head. She edged closer to Sam and whispered urgently, "I'll go back to the house and awaken Tim. You run out to the road and see which direction the van goes. Then we'll get Tim to follow it in his VW."

And without giving her brother a chance to reply, Sara was off on a run across the dark field.

14

The Chase

W AKE up, Tim!" Sara whispered as loudly as she dared
without waking their parents. "I have something important to tell you."

Tim groaned and rolled over. How right Sam was. It was
next to impossible to awaken Tim once he was sound asleep.

Sara drew in a long breath and hissed sharply into his ear,
"Tim, wake up!" She gave his shoulder a hard shake and finally managed to get him to open one eye and sit up in bed.

Before he could drop off to sleep again, she quickly told
what had happened at the shed. By the time she had finished, Tim was wide-awake, his eyes round with excitement.

"Why didn't you wake me when you heard the motorcycle?" he said.

"Are you kidding?" rasped Sara. "By the time we would have gotten you awake, we'd have been too late to have found out what was going on at the shed."

Tim leaped out of bed and rummaged through his desk drawer for his car keys. When he found them, he slipped them into her hands and spoke in a hurry. "Go out to the barn and open the VW, Sara. I'll be down in a jiffy."

Sara's hand tightened around the key ring as she slipped out of the room. Minutes later she had the VW unlocked and was crawling into the passenger seat when Tim appeared in his blue jeans and heavy plaid shirt.

Without a word, he started the jalopy and drove quickly from the barn. Sam's lanky shadow leaped out at them at the end of the driveway. Sara scrambled into the back seat as Sam opened the door and slid in next to Tim.

"Which direction did they go?" asked Tim.

"Up the road," replied Sam. "In the opposite direction from Maplewood."

"How much of a start do they have on us?"

"Not much. I'd say five or ten minutes. Bert must have had quite a time getting Black Cloud into that van without Bob's help. But those minutes waiting for you guys seemed awfully long. I thought you'd never come."

"It was a mammoth task to get old sleepyhead, here, awake," Sara said.

"I can believe that," Sam replied with a grin.

Tim pressed his foot on the accelerator and the jalopy leaped ahead. "Well, five or ten minutes isn't that long a time. Were they going fast?"

"They didn't seem to be," Sam replied. "How fast can a horse van go on a curvy road like this?"

"I'd like to meet the guy who's keeping Huy a prisoner," Tim said fiercely.

"Guys," corrected Sam. "There are two of them in the truck. Bert and the driver, Charlie."

They rode along in tense silence, then Tim said, "Wow, who'd ever think that Bob Dolan was in with this gang of horse thieves. He seemed like such a neat guy." He glanced over at Sam. "Is he the one you suspected?"

Sam nodded silently.

Sara leaned forward and rested her elbows on the back of the front seat. "What made you suspect Bob?"

"Huy's motorcycle," Sam answered simply.

"Huy's motorcycle?" Sara and Tim chimed in together.

"Sure," Sam said. "I figured if Huy was involved in the thefts, he wouldn't go riding up and down the road on that noisy motorcycle, attracting attention to himself, the nights the stallions were stolen."

"So that's why you thought the motorcycle was a decoy," Tim broke in. "Someone wanted to lay the blame on Huy."

"Right," Sam replied "The guilty guy had to be the one using Huy's motorcycle. Therefore, he had to be someone who knew Huy and where he was staying."

"And who knew Huy better than Bob, who worked with him!" exclaimed Sara. "Why didn't I think of that."

Tim replied, "Because we all thought Bob Dolan was such a neat guy."

"Bob knew about the cabin by the pond," Sam went on to explain, "and when he found out that Huy was staying there, he got the idea of using Huy's motorcycle as a decoy."

"How'd he discover Huy was staying at the cabin?" Sara asked.

"Tim and I told him the first day we met him," Sam replied. "You remember, Tim, when we asked Bob if anyone was living in the old cabin."

"Yeah," Tim said slowly. "Now I remember. When Bob

told us nobody was staying there, we told him about finding Huy's motorcycle in the lean-to. That must have given him the idea that Huy was living at the cabin."

"And the idea to use Huy's motorcycle as a decoy, especially since he knew we had seen it," Sam added.

Sara spoke up. "Poor Huy. He never suspected that his motorcycle was being used as a decoy until we told him we heard and saw it the night that Beauty was stolen."

"That's why he denied it," Sam explained. "He really didn't know what went on that night. But after we tipped him off, he probably kept his eyes open for prowlers around the cabin, and tonight when he found his motorcycle missing again, he traced it to the shed. Wow, I'll bet he was as surprised as we were when he saw Bob there!"

"I think I can guess the rest of the mystery," Tim interjected. "Bob had Bert ride the cycle up and down the road while he went to Fox Ridge Farm to get Black Cloud. If anyone was awake at that hour, the motorcycle would attract his attention to the road while Bob was getting the stallion out of the stable. At the same time it would throw suspicion on Huy."

Sam nodded and Tim went on. "Bob rode the stallion along the top of the field, onto the woods road, and up the marked trail we found in our woods the other day. Right?"

"Right," Sam said. "But it's not the end of the mystery. We have to catch up with that van and stop those thieves."

"Easier said than done," Tim muttered with a sigh. "Now that I'm wide-awake and have come to my senses, I'm wondering if we should have called Mr. Raber and the sheriff instead of chasing after those horse thieves by ourselves."

"But we have to help Huy *now*," cried Sara desperately. "If we waited for Mr. Raber and the sheriff, the horse thieves would have had time to get away."

Tim's fingers tightened on the steering wheel. "Well, we haven't caught up with them yet, and I've been pushing this buggy to the speed limit. I don't think a horse van can top that on this road."

Sam, who had been squinting intently at the dark road ahead, suddenly leaned forward, and cried, "Hey, we're coming to another road."

Tim brought the VW to a halt and glanced questioningly to the right and left. "Now which way?"

They had come to an intersection, and the road they had been traveling seemed to dead-end here. The crossroad was more heavily traveled because now and then a car whizzed by. Then something caught Sara's eye. Across from the intersection was an all-night diner, and at the far side of the parking lot, half-hidden in the darkness, was a horse van.

"There they are!" she screeched. "It must be them. Who else would be hauling a horse around this time of night."

"Let's find out," Sam said. "Park as close as you can get to that van, Tim."

Sara sat forward in her seat, her eyes straining through the darkness. She held her breath as she stared at the van. She couldn't see the horse inside because the back was up, hiding it from view. And the cab seemed to be empty. A fearful doubt crept over her. What if this was the wrong van? It had been dark at the shed, and she and Sam hadn't been able to get a very good look at it.

She said close to her twin's ear, "Is it the right one?"

Sam nodded. "It's the right van, all right. I remember the license number."

Sara sank back in her seat with relief and smiled to herself. Leave it to old Sam to think of looking for the license number. He wasn't called Superbrain for nothing.

121

Tim maneuvered the VW at the end of several parked cars, as near as he could get to the horse van. He switched off the engine and said in a low voice, "I'm going to sneak over there and take a look in the cab."

He eased open the door and slipped out into the dimly lighted parking lot. Sam slid out of the VW on the other side, and Sara clambered over the front seat to follow them.

Her throat felt dry and tight as they approached the cab. It still looked empty. She guessed that Bert and the driver, Charlie, were in the diner and Huy was with them.

Tim stepped up on the footboard and peered into the cab. The next moment he jerked open the door, revealing a dark form slumped down in the middle of the front seat.

"Huy!" Tim exclaimed in a hoarse whisper.

The form moved, and the next moment Huy's trembling

Tim jerked open the door of the cab, revealing a dark form slumped down in the middle of the front seat.

voice whispered, "Who is that? Where am I?"

"It's Tim—Tim Harmon. Sara and Sam are with me. You're parked outside a diner, not too far from Maplewood."

With this information, Huy's dark head jerked up. Then in a rasping voice, he gasped, "Help me! Get this thing off my eyes. Hurry!"

While Tim fumbled with the blindfold, Huy blurted out, "Boy, am glad to see you kids. Bert went into diner for cigarettes. Charlie went in after him. Any minute they be back. Hurry!"

Tim finally unknotted the blindfold and helped Huy out of the cab. Sam scooted ahead to open the door to the VW and he literally pushed the Vietnamese boy into the back seat while Tim and Sara scrambled into the front.

Sara looked toward the lighted diner and let out a gasp. "They're coming out. I'm sure that's Bert coming down the steps."

Tim started the engine. "Get down on the floor out of sight, Huy," he warned. He gunned the motor and they tore out of the parking lot.

Peering out of the rear window, Sara glimpsed the two men hurrying toward the horse van. They had just reached it when Tim swung down the road that led to Maplewood and they were out of sight.

"Do you think they'll follow us?" she asked in a shaky voice.

"No way," Tim replied as the dark road stretched ahead of them. "They'll not be going back to the scene of the crime tonight."

Sara glanced back at the boy still squatted on the floor. "Then I guess you can sit up now, Huy," she said.

Sam helped Huy up on the seat beside him. He reached

into his jeans pocket, glad that his old Boy Scout knife was still there. Opening the blade he cut the ropes that bound Huy's wrists together.

Huy let out a deep breath and rubbed the circulation back into his wrists. "Thank you, Sam. Feel much better." With a puzzled frown, he added, "Why Bert and Charlie take me prisoner?"

"Because you know too much," replied Tim. "They would have probably kept you with them until they could get rid of Black Cloud."

"But I know much more now," Huy said. "I listen to them talking. I know where they taking Black Cloud."

Sara swung around in her seat. "You do?" she exclaimed. "Where?"

Huy nodded in the dimness of the car. "Three mile east of place called Blairsville."

"Oh, wow!" Sam cried. "That's important information. Step on it, Tim. We got to let Mr. Raber know and quick."

Fifteen minutes later they were zooming past their own farm and swinging up the lane leading to Fox Ridge Farm. The house and the stable were in darkness. Sara wondered if Bob Dolan was asleep in the tack room.

Tim skidded to a stop at the front of the house, and they got out of the VW and trooped up to the front door. Tim rang the bell several long times before they heard footsteps approaching from inside the house. Presently the porch light flashed on, and the door swung open, framing Mr. Raber in the entranceway. His hair was disheveled from sleep, and he was tucking the top of his pajamas into the back of his trousers as he stared at them.

Sam spoke first. "Mr. Raber, may we come in? We have something important to tell you."

"At this time of night?" the man exclaimed. "Do you

124

know what time it is?" He looked over their shoulders at Huy, who was standing in the shadows. "Is that you, Huy?" he asked with surprise. "What are you doing here with the Harmons?"

"Please, Mr. Raber," Sara broke in. "We can explain everything."

"Well, come in—come in," their neighbor said, stepping aside so they could enter the house.

Taking turns, they quickly told Mr. Raber about what they had discovered that night. When they finished, he frowned deeply and muttered, "I just can't believe that Bob Dolan would do such a thing."

"What do you know about his background?" Tim asked.

"Well—nothing really except that he has had experience with horses and is one of the best trainers I ever had working for me." He shook his head dolefully. "He did tell me once that he wanted to have a stable of his own someday, and I encouraged him."

He paused to collect his thoughts, then his eyes flashing from beneath his bushy brows, he asked, "Where did you hear they were taking Black Cloud?"

"To place three mile east of Blairsville," replied Huy.

"And they have a New Jersey license number," Sam added, rattling off the digits quickly.

"I'll phone the sheriff at once," Mr. Raber said, his face flushed with anger. He left them standing in the hall while he made the call. When he returned, he told them, "Sheriff Marino thinks Bert and Charlie went to the old Blairsville Sportsman's Club that's located three miles east of Blairsville. That old barn and clubhouse are empty, and it's been years since anyone's been back there."

"A good out-of-the-way place to hide stolen horses," Sam mused.

125

Mr. Raber nodded. "The sheriff said he's going to call his deputies, and they are going over there right away to see what's going on." He looked with concern at Huy. "That was a terrible experience for you to go through tonight."

"Well, he's safe now," Sara assured Mr. Raber. "And he won't have to go back to that cabin in the woods tonight. He can stay with us."

The moment she had blurted out those words, she could have bitten her tongue off. She cringed inwardly at the puzzled look on Mr. Raber's face, at her brothers' dark frowns, and at Huy's shocked expression.

Oh, wow, she told herself, what have I done!

15

A Home for Huy

I T had been after midnight when they had slipped into
the house and tiptoed up the back stairs to their rooms.
Tim informed them that, being the oldest, he would assume
the responsibility of telling their parents in the morning
where they had been. Sara knew that Tim wanted to tell it
his own way, but she thought it was generous of him just the
same.

Exhausted from the night's activity, she dropped out of
her clothes and fell into bed. But she found it difficult to
drop off to sleep. She kept thinking of Mr. Raber's last words
before they had left Fox Ridge Farm.

"I believe Huy and I have some serious talking to do,"
Mr. Raber had told them. "I think it's better if he spent the

night here with me at Fox Ridge Farm."

Sara cringed inwardly. She had a pretty good idea what that serious talking would be about. And it was all her fault. If she hadn't forgotten herself and blurted out Huy's secret, he would not have had to confess to Mr. Raber that he had no home in Maplewood but that he had been staying at the cabin by the pond.

Sara let out a long, deep sigh and turned over on her side. What would happen to their Vietnamese friend now? she worried. Would he be sent back to Philadelphia? Back to his sponsors and never be able to see Dzung again? They had solved the mystery of the missing stallions, but, thanks to her, they had failed to help the Vietnamese brothers.

Sam had tried to console her by telling her that Huy was bound to be found out sometime, that he couldn't go on living by himself in that old cabin forever. But that was little consolation for Sara now, and before she finally dropped off to sleep, she said another prayer for Huy and Dzung.

It was Sam's banging on her door the next morning that woke her from a long sleep.

"Do you know what time it is, Twinny?" he said as he burst into her room. "It's ten o'clock. You'd probably sleep the day away if I hadn't awakened you."

"I guess I would," Sara said, yawning. "What's the big rush in getting up?"

Sam walked over to the window and raised the blind so that the morning sun hit Sara square in the eye. With a groan she sat up in bed.

"Mr. Raber telephoned this morning to let us know that Sheriff Marino and his deputies arrested Bert and Charlie. Huy was right. They found them hiding out at the old Blairsville Sportsman's Club."

"Is Black Cloud all right?" Sara asked eagerly.

128

Sam nodded. "They found Black Cloud in the barn there, and he's okay."

"What about Bob Dolan? Did they arrest him, too?"

Sam shook his head. "When the sheriff arrived at Fox Ridge Farm last night and went to the tack room to arrest Bob, Bob was gone. I guess he knew the deal was off and left the farm in a hurry. He's probably miles away by now. But Mr. Raber thinks the sheriff and his men will probably find him, and if they don't, he hopes Bob learned a lesson that crime doesn't pay."

Sam walked back to the door, then turned. "By the way, Sara, Mr. Raber asked us all to come over to Fox Ridge Farm this morning. He has something important to tell us."

Sara shook her head dolefully. "He'll probably tell us that he's turning Huy over to his sponsors in Philadelphia."

"Yeah, I know," Sam said, an expression of worry flitting across his face. "Well, we have to find out sooner or later. Now hurry and get dressed, Sara. You're the last one up."

An hour later they were all gathered in the living room of Fox Ridge Farm. Mr. Raber greeted them with his usual cheerful friendliness and sent Huy into the dining room for extra chairs. Sara was surprised to see Dzung and his foster family sitting on the sofa, all looking as puzzled and expectant as the Harmons.

After they were seated, Mr. Raber cleared his throat and said, "I have brought you here to make an announcement that I believe concerns you all." He turned and smiled at Huy. "Huy Chau has consented to be my foster son."

For a moment everyone was too surprised to speak. Sara's heart spiraled with joy. When she found the words to express her feelings, she exclaimed, "Oh, Mr. Raber, that's super!"

Tim, smiling broadly, pommeled Huy on the shoulder, and Sam grinned his crooked grin. Professor Harmon and

129

Jim Burton congratulated Mr. Raber, but it was Dzung, happiest of all, who leaped up from the sofa and ran over to his brother and hugged him.

When all the happy excitement calmed down, Mr. Raber explained, "Last night Huy and I had a long talk. He told me that he and Dzung are brothers and how, before they had left Vietnam, they had promised their grandmother that they would stay together. He told me how he had left his sponsors in Philadelphia and had hidden out in that old cabin by the pond so that he could be near Dzung."

He paused and looked blissfully at his audience. "Well, this morning I called my wife and daughter in Nebraska, and we all agreed that we would like to have Huy in our family. So the next thing I did was to call his sponsors in Philadelphia. They were relieved to hear that he is safe and well and do not see any difficulties in Huy becoming our foster son."

Mr. Raber looked fondly at the Vietnamese boy. "I have always wanted a son, Huy, and now that Bob Dolan is gone, I'll need you more than ever."

"I work hard and be good son," Huy said eagerly.

"Oh, it won't be all work," Mr. Raber replied with a twinkle. "I plan to hire another hand to take Bob's place in the fall when you'll be going to school."

"School!" Huy exclaimed and made a funny face.

They all laughed. Tim said, "I know what you mean, Huy."

All this while the Burtons had been sitting quietly on the sofa, taking everything in. Now Jim Burton leaned forward and cleared his throat. "I have something to say to Huy," he announced.

They all looked expectantly at the young professor who turned his attention to the Vietnamese boy, his smile both wide and warm. "Like your grandmother, Huy, I believe that you and Dzung should be together as much as possible, so I want you to feel free to come to our house to be with Dzung anytime you wish."

"Oh, yes!" agreed Mrs. Burton, smiling happily at Huy. "We are so glad you found your brother. Please consider our house your second home."

Dzung looked up at his foster parents, his serious brown eyes shining gratefully. Huy's face shone, too, with happiness. He stood up and bowed the low, gracious Vietnamese bow. "Thank you. You make Dzung and me very happy."

A moment later his smile faded, and he shifted uneasily from one foot to the other. "Will return blanket and pillow Dzung took for me," he said. "Will pay for canned food and pan to cook in."

The Burtons looked puzzled at first, then Jim Burton burst out laughing. "Now we know, Julie, where the bedding and canned food suddenly disappeared to."

Huy turned to his brother with a serious look. "We live in America now, Dzung. No more have to be afraid. No more sticky fingers—no more lies."

Dzung nodded soberly. As Huy's voice trailed off into silence, Sam reached into his pocket and drew out a large handkerchief with flashy red and black squares on it.

"That reminds me," he said. "I have something that doesn't belong to me, either." Handing Mr. Raber the handkerchief, he added, "I believe this is yours, sir."

"My favorite handkerchief!" Mr. Raber exclaimed with surprise. "Where did you find it?"

"Sara found it in our shed where the stallions were kept," Sam replied.

Mr. Raber looked down at the handkerchief with a puzzled frown. And then his voice tightened. "It seems as if Bob

131

planted a clue to involve even me."

"Or else to throw us off our suspicions when Sara found that bridle in the shed," Sam said quickly.

Sara intervened with a question. "Why was Bob involved with the horse thefts? He seemed like such a nice person. And he liked horses."

"He liked horses and was a good trainer," Mr. Raber said, shaking his head sadly. "When the sheriff questioned Bert and Charlie last night, they confessed everything. To get a lighter sentence, I suppose. Anyway, they said that Bob was offered a lot of money for helping to steal thoroughbreds. Bob had often spoken about owning his own stable, but that takes money. I guess the temptation was too much for him."

"Did the sheriff find the man who operates the ring of horse thieves?" Professor Harmon asked.

Mr. Raber nodded. "Yes, he has a big stable in New Jersey. The stolen horses were kept at the old Blairsville Sportsman's Club until it was safe to move them. Then they were taken to New Jersey and sold to unsuspecting buyers. Early this morning the man was arrested and his stable impounded. Fortunately, Beauty and White Lightning hadn't been sold yet, so we'll get them back. Black Cloud was returned to my stable this morning."

"Well, that's good news," Mrs. Harmon said.

Mr. Raber clapped his freckled hands on his knees. "Any more questions?" he asked, looking around the room.

When they shook their heads, he beamed gratefully at the young people. "Then I have just one more thing to add," he said. "I want to thank you all for being such good friends. Without your detective work and courage, I might not have gotten back my American Saddlebreds."

He paused and winked over at Sara. "And if a certain little lady, out of the kindness of her heart, hadn't let the cat

132

out of the bag last night, I might not have known about Huy, and he might not have been my foster son."

Sam and Tim grinned over at Sara, and Huy gave her a big smile. Sara sighed with relief. Everything seemed to be working out just right.

Mr. Raber rose from his chair and put a hand on Huy's shoulder. "Why don't we show these folks what good cooks we are, son. What do you say we go outside to the barbecue and grill them some steaks?"

"Okay by me, Dad," Huy said brightly.

"I help," Dzung piped up in all seriousness. "I better cook than Huy."

Mr. Raber laughed and took the small boy's hand. "Come along then."

"And we women will toss a salad," Mrs. Harmon offered. "Just show us your kitchen, Ed."

Later as they were eating delicious steaks and a tossed salad, Huy and Dzung came over to where Sara and Sam were sitting on the grass, their plates of food propped on their knees.

"Dzung wants me to go to church with him this Sunday," Huy told them.

"That's great," Sam said. "Are you going?"

Huy put an arm around his small brother and nodded. "I want your God to be my friend, too. I want to thank him for answering Sara's prayers for me."

Sam looked at his sister and one corner of his mouth tilted into a smile. Sara smiled back.

"Even though God does it in ways we sometimes least expect, he always answers our prayers," she said happily.

133

Ruth Nulton Moore was born in Easton, Pennsylvania. She received a B.A. degree from Bucknell University and an M.A. from Columbia University. She did postgraduate work in education at the University of Pittsburgh.

Mrs. Moore taught English and social studies in schools in Pennsylvania and Michigan. Along with producing poetry and stories for children's magazines, she has written twelve juvenile novels. Several of her books have been translated into other languages and sell in England, Sweden, Finland, and Puerto Rico, as well as in the United States and Canada.

Mrs. Moore lives in Bethlehem, Pennsylvania, with her husband who is a professor of accounting at Lehigh University. They have two grown sons and a granddaughter.

When she is not at her typewriter, Mrs. Moore is busy lecturing about the art of writing to students in public schools and colleges in her area.

Mrs. Moore is a member of the Children's Authors and Illustrators of Philadelphia. Her biography appears in *The International Authors and Writers Who's Who*, 1982, and *Pennsylvania Women in History*, 1983.

Moore's children's novel, *Danger in the Pines* (Herald Press), received the C. S. Lewis Honor Book Medal as one of the top five children's books with a Christian message published in 1983.